© Vytenis Rožukas
El.p. vytenis.rozukas@gmail.com

Spausdino UAB "Biznio mašinų kompanija"
J.Jasinskio g. 16 a, Vilnius LT-01112
Tel. 8 5 254 69 64
Faksas 8 5 254 69 62

Order this book online at www.trafford.com
or email orders@trafford.com

Most Trafford titles are also available at major online book retailers.

Printed in the United States of America.

ISBN: 978-1-4251-8389-9 (Softcover)
ISBN: 978-1-4269-8808-0 (e-Book)
ISBN: 978-1-4669-4999-7 (Audio)

Trafford rev. 11/04/2013

 www.trafford.com

North America & international
toll-free: 1 888 232 4444 (USA & Canada)
fax: 812 355 4082

HORIZONS OF TRANSCENDENTAL IDEALISM

film novel
Vytenis Rožukas

RUSSIAN

(Re: Jagger, Mick)

Russsssians. Rhlitle baby, eat volf beforrre volf get chens to eat you.

Vilnius, 2007

Foreword

In my pack of cards: Jagger's daughter like the Siamese twin Annette, or the Siamese twin — the girl from America. Jagger or an actor who looks like Jagger, Charlie Watts or an actor who looks like Charlie Watts, P. McCartney or an actor who looks like P. McCartney and so on for Sean Lennon, Rod Stewart, Cat Stevens, David Bowie and Jonas Mekas, Jurga Ivanauskaitė and Peter Handke.

The Siamese twin Annette is the prototypical girl from America — all computer graphics plus the art of the made-to-order dressmaker.

In this parody there is some truth: about fifty-fifty. I am a scout for the chaos of multifaceted reality. Such is the artist's mission. Risk and hassles notwithstanding.

❀ ❀ ❀

A special thank you to the doctors of Germany, each one of you individually, and to Dr Annette — personally ...

Dotted lines 10-12 of the new ideology. Vytenis Rožukas' maxims, mind technique and convenient life map, easy to refer to, easy to plan each day with. This book includes Ringo Starr's primary school.

Contents

The wealthiest philanthropists in the world, old rockers and literati (J. Ivanauskaitė, P. Handke, P. McCartney, M. Jagger, C. Watts, K. Richards, D. Bowie, R. Stewart, J. Mekas) establish an Empire of Art in the Munich suburb of Haare. Pooling their talents they decide to examine some of the ills troubling the world: the issues of Arabs and immigration, and the problems of militarism.

After M. Jagger and P. McCartney we see the Siamese twin Annette, who has two passports (she got an *approbatur* — permission from the pope). Annette is Rudolf Hess' granddaughter. A super family doing humanitarian work.

This screenplay was written by a whole heap of writers who were participants on the "Europa 2000" Lisbon — Saint Petersburg Literary Express. They wove in the horror elements.

Re: Jagger

Anna from Saint Petersburg
(5. Love, sympathy, friendship)
(Written by the Spaniard.)

Tall girl—a Tartar. Without fear of being wrong I can say that this one is a definite possibility; the scent of Polish perfume, sharp and sweet and never boring, not overpowering, clean. I was her first love. She is in the top five of my great loves. The only reason I didn't marry her is because she is a noisy eater.

A modest girl, loving, sensible, a very good tailor, she made me a shirt with four pockets, which I have kept through all the vicissitudes of my life and I still have now. One time I nearly burst from laughter when she came out of the shower with my platform shoes, naked, hiding herself with a towel. I will never forget how another time, without any coaching from me, she hid from the administrator of the Astoria Hotel and we snuck off, after having had the opportunity to enjoy some lovemaking.

With a flower in my teeth, my memory tells the truth from the album of 111 people I have been closely involved with, an album that all we mortals have. My women. Anna from Saint Petersburg. Cows moo as they give milk; I am mooing as I pour out my heart. My treasure, in the blue sky, hanging from the edge of a star, I send you a kiss. There is no better dream.

I chatted her up at the bus station. She was coming back from her native land, along the rugged shoreline of the Volga, where trees snooze and Pan sleepily plays his hypocritical song.

Eternal fiancée, never becoming the wife, I asked her whether anyone had told her how attractive she was, the dear seamstress? May I invite you to coffee, tea, maybe we can go dancing or something..?

—How do you prefer it, she asked, eyes open or closed? as she stared at me as if I had grown another nose.

—I know your type, Don Juan, and every time after one of these encounters I have to buy myself a new head.

—I can cry a little, I said, and we can continue this in a bar. Bars are all the same, from Paris to the empty plains of Texas.

She parted with her innocence in the Astoria Hotel very reluctantly, very slowly, like drowning a beloved puppy dog.

Mama spider comes back to the dusty corner and grimaces to frighten me.

❋ ❋ ❋

—Are you frightened, little girl? Keith Richards asked the girl.
—I am, the girl replied. It's one of the worst moments in the life of every woman.

❋ ❋ ❋

(Written by the Englishman.)

We met a week later in an overpacked Saint Petersburg café, where the Russian girls from her female-dominated flats were surprised that I didn't switch over to European sex standards. Love is like a wooden bridge with rotten

3

beams—you have to cross it very carefully. I kissed her breasts and her mouth, a cool grape. Such silence, you think you can hear the moon tapping on the windowpane. It is snowing.

—Have I told you that I love you? I asked.

—It's dangerous, she says. I might die laughing. Tell me that I'm not at home.

With a pat on the shoulder, the Lord goes on his way, off into the bronze sunset...

We fall into a sweet sleep.

The bus is on its way to the airport. As we say goodbye I draw words on the window of the bus. There is fear in her eyes, although she is laughing.

The soul of a person is that person's image in the eyes of others. (B.P.)

On this item the General is the one who has tried heroine and cocaine. We Rolling Stones are, or were, kings in this category, while a breastfeeding infant is a Sergeant.

To retain an ideal in all the labyrinths of hedonism is very difficult. That is a complicated and tricky question. I was happy with Anna from Saint Petersburg.

(Re: 8. Beauty, imagination, romanticism)

Author's voice, part Stirlitz, part Sorge:

Maybe you have heard about the "Europa 2000" Literary Express train that went from Lisbon to Madrid, Lyons, Paris, Munich, Berlin — and all the way to Saint Petersburg. Ten of the best writers were chosen, and ten translators who translate into English, and lots were drawn to decide who would write first, because the beginning shapes the idea and the subject of the screenplay, and the one who goes first has the greatest influence on it. The first lot was drawn by the Lithuanian, but the group decided that this would be a screenplay for a horror movie, which — they say — will give even the most jaded consumer of culture goose bumps, so we let the first chapter be written by a Spaniard, a true admirer of the horror genre. The Lithuanian got to the next chapter, Chapter Two. Each author writes a chapter. When all have had their turn, the ending will be written by the Spaniard or the Lithuanian.

The assembly of *literati* decided to go for a high level scenario: with the help of philanthropists, the big names of the performing arts and politics, millionaires and billionaires, a resort would be purchased and there the Empire of Art would be established, a State like the Vatican, Luxembourg, San Marino. Once the real estate is purchased it well be self-supporting, assisted by the world's richest performers and artists, and their fans. Why rock stars? Because Paul McCartney, Mick Jagger, Charlie Watts, Rod Stewart and David Bowie have all had nose jobs, which cost millions. The ingenious surgeon devised it

4

that their sense of smell is now as keen as that of a wild beast in the forest. Accompanied by parapsychological powers and super abilities in rational thought. Because they are the richest people in the entertainment world, followed by filmmakers.

Philanthropists can influence politicians and world leaders, because they also have a non-self-interested devotion to artistic masterpieces. There is no formal bureaucracy, which would sink any creative project. Capitalist private initiative can achieve more than socialist attempts at problem solving by members of the government who in any case have a lower IQ than do rock geniuses. The latter have overcome challenges in one area, so they can overcome challenges in other areas too. They have learned music well, they can learn anything.

That is why the group of *literati* chose the medley of rock stars and philanthropists.

They hope to get assistance in buying the *Druskininkai* resort from the Government of Lithuania, and they hope to get donations from the whole world, from the UN, from UNESCO. Quite possible, because a watchful eye is being kept on the activities of the Empire of Art by its owners — Paul McCartney, Mick Jagger, Ringo Starr, etc.

There are a lot of problems in the world. Every day 240,000 people die of starvation. But at the meeting of authors on the Literary Express, only three problems were chosen: Arabs, immigration and Russians. With shy or eloquent IQs they will solve the problems on paper. There is no time, time stands still while you do your exercises on 11 exercise machines (an English idea, called Ringo Starr's Mental Technique) and you travel through the little segment of time that is allotted to you — 50 years, 80 years. Sleep, activity, thought and life — that's Hotel Earth, we organise it together and care for it and we are all kindred.

2. One of us, not one of us
(10. Good name)

The secrets of the Empire of Art will be passed by word of mouth, like recipes for wine or cognac, which have been passed down from their first formulators.

Ringo Starr's Primary School
A film novel

authors: a Spaniard, a Lithuanian, a Pole, an Englishman,
an Arab, a Jew, a Russian, an American, a Georgian, a German
and again — two Lithuanians (male and female)

(8. Beauty, terror, imagination)
(Written by the Spaniard)

Chapter I

— How's that? I never told you about Annette? She is outrageously beautiful. She is the fuehrer of the Empire of Art, with two heads and two legs, like a girl, an American prototype. Very pretty, she won the university beauty contest (no other Siamese twins presented themselves). Her grandfather was the Germans' holy martyr — Rudolf Hess. And this is not dreamed up just because it sounds interesting.

— And who are you, to think that you have the right to speak? — asked the girl, approaching the campfire in the night.

— I'm Keith Richards. And what are you doing here?

— I'm travelling the world looking for horror. I'm enjoying this campfire. Look at those two sets of gallows with sexy-voiced creatures; the gallows creak, shadows flicker in the light of the campfire, all around are corpses, like that one in the coffin there — warming up by the fire, jaws moving, like he doesn't want to rot, moulder away ... Spectres with worm-eaten lips. It's great, but do you have any stories that would really scare me? I mean, the whole world knows about McCartney's special olfactory talents. Tell me something about that.

Keith Richards patted the girl's head and said:

— I have an idea how to earn millions from art. We have studied the idea carefully and set some guidelines. Me, Jagger and Watts, and Bill Gates.

— On your right is the Russian-speaking Grim Reaper, it won't let me lie. I'll tell you about the Siamese twin Annette. A horror story. It will be both painful and easy to contemplate. Let's have a plaintive chorus of mezzo-soprano witches to accompany the rock stars' and philantropists' journey; and as for this medley of rock stars and philantropists' — let's use it to convince everyone that only talented and very rich people can change the world. If Paganini were alive now as a rich person, he would use his talents, his wealth and his passion for the violin to solve the problem of emigration; trust me, the problem would be solved. The ideology of a hundred fun movies would change people's attitude to emigration. I'm getting worked up like a *Metropolitan Opera* debutante. Let's have some flamenco music to accompany my story, while you try to shave with the blades of my text's fantasies.

Annette

(Re: 8. Beauty, horror)

A church. Doves against a background of a black sun. A priest is reciting prayers and joining in matrimony the young German Siamese twin Annette Hess with both Mick Jagger and olfactory superman Paul McCartney. Special dispensation has been obtained from the Pope (a German). P. McCartney smelled some asbestos in the church, and the scent of the priests interred there, remnants of the Catholic network, and Annette's pleasant, sharp scent, the scent of the dust of eternity and a good aura.

— Enough horror? — Keith Richards asked the girl. The campfire crackles and warms those nearby. The corpses are very interested in it.

— Yes, — said the girl. — It's ghastly. But not unbearable. I want more cause for oohs and ahs in the rest of the story. I want to be scared out of my wits. That's why I left home.

✻ ✻ ✻

The English Club

(Re: 10. Good reputation)
(Written by the Lithuanian)

Fencing practice. This type of physical training activity is a prestige sport nowadays, and Charlie Watts, the drummer of the Rolling Stones, is crossing rapiers with his boss — Mick Jagger. One smells blueberries, and the other (M. Jagger) — a bit of manure from the spring manuring of the fields that is going on. This is a smell he recognises, reminding him as it does of excessive accolades.

— The shit is good this morning and the day has started well, — says Jagger. — I think I'll win. Charlie, you're no match for me.

— It's a scandal, truly a scandal, — says Prince Charles in the dressing room with his sparring partner Paul McCartney, as they rested after a good workout.

— You, Paul, can feel as proud as a Vatican cat. You sense the world through your nose. Doing battle with a left-hander is a difficult and tricky matter. You were born for the rapier. Your magnificent sense of smell has trained you to get the scent. After a bout of this sport, some remarkable smells come to you, and through the cracks in your thoughts many ideas fall through, a good half-kilogram of idea-raisins.

7

— Prince, — says P. McCartney, — our grandchildren will see the day when war and weapons such as cannons, rockets, pistols and machine guns will all be just sport, a harmless and safe mode of self-expression. In the time of D'Artagnan people died in duels, but not any more. Similarly, after a few centuries, death in battle will be pushed right off the menu of civilisation by legislation and social fashion. The billions now wasted on weapons will be saved to be spent on the poor and the weak, because the strong will look after those in a lower social category. I smell the future. It smells like a girl getting her first period.

— It's a nail in the coffin still on the coffin upholsterer's lips, — says the prince, — such being the blight of our time, which you can see from the newspapers. I'm talking about the emigration issue. The immigrant has to answer. Did we invite you? Are you our guest? If not, go home and get off our backs. The English Club should solve this problem. It's a fact that Jagger is more capable than Blair, the hired British problem-solver, whereas Bill Gates, who started off in life with the seat of his trousers wearing thin, is more capable than George Bush. They are more capable and cannot be bribed. All we need is for them to be interested. I'll give 20 million, to be spent on art and ideology, because I am convinced that only IQ determines success in matters that require intellectual prowess.

Jagger too, having finished his duels, goes to join the tea-drinkers. Likewise Charlie Watts.

(9. Leading the field, prestige)

— I have an idea how to milk some millionaires, says Watts. — I smell big money. It's the smell of the big porker that is going to feed many people, the smell of her pigpen, also the smell of a swallow that has flown over and shit on the brim of a Jew's homburg. The English Club is a gathering of top experts, and with an injection of 20 million in funds, it could earn billions. We have seed money, ingenuity and contacts. We can achieve. Politicians — they're like apes trying to play chess.

— They do not have a rich experience of life, not to mention education or the ability to think independently.

(10. Good reputation)

— Your offer,- said Mick Jagger to prince Charles, — stuck to Watts and me like chewing gum on the seat of an economy class railway carriage. I smell an old good-quality leather valise, and the smell of the captain's cabin on an ocean liner with ten decks. What better to invest in than the creation of the Empire of Art? All we need to do is choose a place. Today it would cost about four hundred million. In fifty years its value will double. We will resolve the issue of good reputation once and for all. After a couple of centuries Jagger's name will not be Sarah Bernhardt, but Socrates, which is three stars higher in the catalogue of good reputations. The aroma will be of rose petal essence — the Bulgarians used to make perfume like that. It reminds me of a similar smell I have in my memory: the aroma of a village milkmaid smelling like milk.

* * *

Centre Georges Pompidou in Paris. Near the entrance is a raised platform for the duel with rapiers. All month long the media has been talking about the forthcoming duel between Bill Gates and Paul McCartney, and bets are being placed. Most people bet on P. McCartney. It is being emphasised that P. McCartney is left-handed.

The area was fenced off and tickets were being sold. The TV companies have paid millions for the rights to film the event.

— Gentlemen, — says Bill Gates after the duel, — both I and P. McCartney have earned our money honestly, without speculation or fraud. We have collected a couple of million, and as much again will be contributed by Gates and McCartney, and all the money will go to children suffering from cancer, so that their short lives could at least be happier.

(8. Beauty, fantasy)

— Maestro, — says Jonas Mekas, godfather of John Lennon's son Sean and creator of the movie "Imagine" at the banquet after the duel, on the subject of the Empire of Art. — I know where a good location for it would be. Jews from all around spend their holidays in Druskininkai. Jews are the world's thermometers. They have a particular nature and aura. The collection of sanatoriums and rest homes in Druskininkai would really suit people in my line of work. Their talents would work for the benefit of humanity and for the benefit of their own quality of life. Druskininkai is easy to fall in love with. That is no lowbrow holiday resort. The Jews realised that long ago. Geniuses like Jacques Lipchitz, Konstantinas Čiurlionis, Chaim Soutine. In Druskininkai there is a Spring Poetry Festival, and an Autumn Prose Festival ... Druskininkai — it's a ten-carat diamond, a gem of nature. The "Father of Lithuania" — the Nemunas River — flows through it, as does the feisty young Ratnyčėlė River. Čiurlionis "Forest" symphony epitomises in music the essence of a forest. And what is art? In my opinion, it is attempting to transmute into gold the morning dew on a blanket left out all night. The trumpets of the golden sun sparkle on the dewy grass on the banks of the Nemunas, where the distant past reverberates through the haze of time.

(Re: 10. Good reputation)

Lithuanian girls are beautiful, part of Lithuania's natural beauty. The warriors of the past fought to defend that beauty. They occupied Russia as far as Smolensk, and reached the Black Sea. They were not usurpers: they gathered the tribute, but allowed the Slavs to live the way they wanted to. On the other hand, when the Russians occupied Lithuania they gained a dreadful reputation. Take a swab from history and you will know a nation's mentality. A shaft of sunlight plays on dust specks in the air; the blood-like smell of newly mown grass stimulates those who enjoy life.

— Lithuanians don't like Russians, - says prince Charles. In yesterday's newspaper I read about a Russian getting done in, here in London. They cut off his head and left a message: "Holidaying in Vilnius". Today another Russian corpse and another note: "Holidaying in Vilnius".

(Re: 2. One of us, not one of us)

— In a public toilet in Palanga, - says Jonas Mekas, — I saw written on the wall „давить лабусов" — a Russian message suggesting that those who say "Labas" [Lithuanian for "Hello"] should be crushed. Lithuanians ingest a dislike of Russians with their mother's milk. If you don't eat the wolf, the wolf will eat you. I will ask Sean to organise a massacre of the Russians. There will be a scandal, an outcry in the press, and the message will be out that Russians needn't try to come to Lithuania, because the people there are odious Mongol — Tartars. After implementing this idea we can put out the word that it was just a joke, just a bit of black humour.

(10. Good reputation)

— Gentlemen, — Bill Gates told BBC television, — listen to what my Lithuanian friend Jonas Mekas has to say, he may know something about the murder of former Russian KGB agent Litvinenko in London. I don't get involved in politics, but it does surprise me to see the Russians murdering each other, and it would be interesting to know what the true background to these events is. I also send my greetings to the Head of the Russian Secret Police.

At this point Bill Gates dropped his trousers and bared his behind. There were guffaws and applause to accompany this scene.

Meanwhile, Jonas Mekas said:

It's really true that personal self-expression is like nationalism, with the difference that a good reputation is not necessarily earned by exercising force. There are various highways and byways that one can travel on the road to

10

building a good reputation for one's nation. Limit force to sport, avoiding the criminality of militarism. I am against knocking off Russians in the capital cities of the world. But maybe it will frighten off the uninvited guests. In Latvia and Estonia the Russians were colonisers and they continue to be.

Yesterday a KGB man expounded to me: "Take medicine — half the nurses in Lithuania are Russian. They wouldn't so much as help a Lithuanian cure a wart on his finger. A Russian doctor's heart is filled with joy when she can do some harm to a Lithuanian." Hatred begets hatred. You post something from the Post Office, the KGB man who has been working there since time immemorial inspects it. He'll confiscate your letter if he detects in it anything that portrays Lithuania in a good light to other Europeans.

The taxi drivers in Vilnius are all Russians. They keep an eye on the more talented people. A colleague of mine in the Writer's Club had a run-in with a KGB spy, "Mary the Snitch". She collected the information, and if necessary, the victim would be assassinated. Jurga Ivanauskaitė, a writer, because she wrote a daring novel about Russian fifth columnists — she was irradiated, got sick with cancer, and died. Beresnevičius was also murdered just as soon as it become clear that he had great talent. He was murdered on his way home from the Writers' Union café, where, by the way, the owner, a KGB spy, and his Russian barmaids were insisting on playing loud Russian music although it was Lithuanian Independence Day, 16 February.

In the hospital, in a café, these mysterious 'friends' appear who want to chat you up. They are secret agents. A Lithuanian is afraid to speak freely, he trembles at the thought that the Russians might return one day.

I worked it out for myself: half my mail never gets to me.

The only concept of 'good reputation' a Russian understands is if you praise them, kowtow to them. All that dates back to the Tsarist era.

My brother's flat was carpeted by a builder who is a former Security official. He mixed arsenic into the glue.

The politics of brute force, a criminal outlook, contempt for those who keep their self-respect — these are the Russians' achievements. To them a person is like a fly: squash it if you have to.

We know what secret police collaborators are like in those places where there is no democracy and the press is muzzled. That is the spirit of the foetid jail. For some reason that's how Russians understand 'a good reputation'. Tell me, what's the background of their current President? He comes from the KGB, more of all the cunning rats and lowlifes.

That Russian, the KGB man with a limp, he threatened me. He accused me of having knowledge about who was organising the decapitation of Russians.
***

(Horror, beauty, fantasy)

Campfire, gallows.
The girl was watching Keith Richards, transfixed.

— Here's that heap of Russian heads, - says Keith Richards, — all with a label "On holiday in Vilnius".

— I'm not at all terrified, — says the girl.

More flamenco music. Keith continues his story about Annette.

— Dear little one, — he says, — only criminals, philanthropists and artists are free. We want to clean out all the banks associated with art and politics.

***

— Solomon was an ingenious solver of olympian problems, — said Jonas Mekas as the old rocker drank tea in the English Club after fencing.

— This time without sugar? — asked Paul. The smell of this room is particularly dear to me. It's in the top ten of good smells that I am familiar with.

— For the sugar to dissolve you have to stir it, but I'm for total freedom: I won't even be a servant for myself, — said Jonas Mekas.

– I truly am the only one that's really free, — said Bill Gates. He approached a map of the world, shut his eyes and stabbed the map with a ballpoint pen, not knowing where the pen would land.

— New Zealand, — said Jonas Mekas.

— I will donate 15 million dollars to the New Zealand Labour Party. What do you think: will the Government be loyal to me? This is how to make a difference in the world.

(Meals, sleep, clothes, transport)

— Sean Lennon has already been in jail for a week, — says Watts. — In Augsburg. As I think about him I can smell the lamb kebabs Stalin's cook used to prepare for him, splashed with white Georgian wine from the vineyards of Batumi. He snoozes in a sitting position, propped up against the door of his cell. Every night he hears the gurneys trundle along the corridor to the operating theatre. They quash your conviction or reduce the length of your sentence if you surrender a kidney or part of your liver. Those who are caught without passports are carved up into little bits. Sean intimated to us that there may be fans that would be willing to pay big money to buy the kidneys, liver or heart of John Lennon's son. It's a prestige thing. Death? No, it's easier to live. We have to do something for Sean. A strange smell, I sense unease, this smell revolts me as much as a conviction for an unspeakable crime. Everything in life can be bought, except IQ and beauty. We must do something for Sean.

— I have a candidate, — says Paul McCartney, — for the Congress of the Empire of Art. It's Annette Hess, Rudolf Hess' granddaughter, author of the novel "Hieroglyphs of the Beatle Era". That's the very best novel of the post-Salinger era. Its bouquet of aromas — lilacs in bloom on a humid spring evening, linden blossoms in summer, and a hint of acrid cat's piss. Its success in Europe and America too is a hopeful sign. She is a fine candidate for the post of

12

cultural fuehrer. If Jagger or I were to get that post, we wouldn't have the same drive. Besides, Nazi gold stashes in Swiss banks are a considerable motivation.

— She's locked up in a psychiatric hospital, — said Jagger, — Haare, near Munich. It gives off the smell of a zoo, particularly the lynx's lair, and the smell of a chicken scalded with boiling water. She has been accused of nationalist propaganda. Her lawyers got her out of jail and into a psychiatric hospital. A bit of a sham, really. She's allowed out to go to a café in the nearest Munich suburb. We just need to put a campaign bus there with equipment in it and we can be candidates, offering solutions to the problems of emigration, the Arabs and the Russians. We'll keep in contact with those who have had super nose jobs: Rod Stewart, David Bowie, Paul McCartney, Sean Lennon and you, Your Majesty Prince Charles, who even without the operation already had a powerful sense of smell. The Russian problem is the same problem that existed in Nazi Germany, where citizen no. 1 denounced citizen no. 2, who in turn denounced citizen no. 3, who was meanwhile busy denouncing citizen no. 1 — a totalitarian spying and snitching system. The Russians use it everywhere, especially in countries that were formerly part of the USSR, where every third person is an informant. The Russians are never stingy about spending money on war or spying. The Russian's espionage intelligence leads the world, and their military officers are the best in the world.

— A joke. What did the clock's long hand say to the short hand? — asked Prince Charles.

— That in one hour he would wet his jacket with the tears streaming from his eyes. They will be tears of joy, great joy, — said Charlie Watts. — We have thought up a great scheme and we will empty out the World Bank without risking our lives or freedom. But still it's not enough for me. I'm thinking about my great great grandchildren. With my whole body I sense the invigorating feel of a rain-wetted field of rye, and the smell of a dusty road that has just been rained on. Those to me are like visions of the future.

(1. Meals, sleep, clothes)

Sean was playing with a hose in the jail yard. A complex smell of Kaiser's barracks and cheap eau de cologne. Maybe even the smell of clotted blood. Yoko Ono had also arranged a nose operation for Sean. The warder kept looking at that oxygen thief as if he had a vestal virgin standing next to him.

Twelve o'clock was approaching.

— If you don't want to be afraid of the shower, — said the Turk in an oversweet cello-like voice, — leave the steel with me and walk around in circles.

With some bread they had, the prisoners were feeding the pigeons, which are not prisoners but are free to take wing and fly, up over the high fences and away.

The Sun does not know that it is the Sun, it just shines without knowing what it's doing.

(10. Good reputation)

A free person does not know that he is free, although kindergarten, school, university, work, family life — they are all muzzles that interfere with chewing; but one gets used to them. Life is good; you just have to get used to it and figure it all out.

Author's voice, baritone, part Stirlitz, part Sorge.

(10. Good reputation)

Ringo Starr, Beatles drummer, thought up the Ringo Starr Periodic Table:
1. Meals, clothes, sleep, transport, domestic requirements.
2. One of us, not one of us, keeping up with the peer group, *fait social* — customs, house.
3. Hedonism, happiness, comfort.
4. Profession, hobby, sport, culture, tourism.
5. Love, sympathy, friendship.
6. Family, children, parents.
7. Catharsis.
8. Beauty, fantasy, horror, imagination, romance.
9. Being first in every competition.
10. Good reputation, a posthumous good reputation in the big apartment building that we call the Earth, a total assessment in relation to all our education and experience.
11. A plan, a system, a mistake, no mistake, a mathematically precise setting of our life plan.
12. Freedom, games.

This 12-category mental gymnastics formula is Ringo Starr's periodic table, which is taught in sects, and in Ringo Starr Primary Schools under the direction of Mick Jagger. By the way, this idea comes from an English author. I, as a Lithuanian, think it's a successful practical philosophy: what you desire, fervently desire, you will get.

Sean Lennon was thinking about Ringo, who was loved by all the world. He wanted to continue John's ideas, but he didn't know how. Maybe it's because rock and roll, which has the smell of good cognac when you break out a very subtly flavoured cheese to go with it and you see the dew on the very fine hairlets of a girl's whiskers, is already in the past, like the tango. Another

14

revolutionary movement — maybe one for an ideology of Muslim - Christian - Judaic unity might do it, but that is not in sight yet.

(1. Transport)

In the jail yard Sean heard the throb of the descending helicopter. Its door flew open and a couple of gymnastic rings dangled just above him. Everyone knew that Sean practised gymnastics even more than karate.

And now he demonstrated what he could do. The helicopter is high, the stakes are high and he is at the height of his youth.

Flooring two Turks, kicking himself free of a Ukrainian (jail is full of immigrants), Sean grips the gymnastic rings and he even formed a cross. The prisoners in the jail yard whooped and clapped.

Sean was now free, and he knew that he was free. As John said — absolute freedom.

The prison warders did not make much effort to stop him. Privately each one of them loved John and Yoko's son.

(9. Being first in every competition)

A Munich court. The smell of mouse shit, signifying strength and fertility, and adaptation — which commands respect, and aggressiveness: such are the smells. On the defendant's bench sits Sean. His speech was quoted by all the planet's newspapers, and Jonas Mekas was right. For some centuries now Russia will miss out on providing a protectorate for Lithuania, because Lithuanians' feelings for Russia are evident for all to see. The USA and Germany are very happy about the reestablishment of Baltic sovereignty, so near and dear to the spirit of Lincoln and Washington.

There is a little forest creature that fouls the air so badly that none of its predators will chase it.

On this occasion the Lithuanians have behaved according to this strategy.

Sean admitted that his links with terrorists where a bluff, in order to find something out about them. He only knows Lithuanians to the extent that they used to visit John Lennon. Those were Jonas Mekas and Jurgis Mačiūnas.

An alibi was guaranteed.

The German security agents commenced an investigation into human organ transplants exploiting the hopeless situation of emigrants, and not just emigrants.

But private work is one thing, while being obliged to do something by pressure from above is an entirely different thing. There is also the question of peer group. Jailbirds don't usually sell out each other, and besides, they are involved and dirty.

— Half of every day I don't struggle, I don't race, I just live for my own pleasure, — says Sean, — but just half, twelve hours, and I try to get more pleasure. Saturday, Sunday — no exceptions. I'm a fighter. I have Bobby

15

Fisher's courage and dedication. The other twelve hours I dedicate to that eleven level Ringo Starr Periodic Table system. That's the next morning's activity. It has the smell of a street being asphalted, when the asphalt is still steaming hot under the roller, redolent of hope and security ... and a touch of the smell of mist from the evening's condensation, rising off the lawns. Unfortunately, my surgeon died and took the secret to his grave with him. Only a few of us rockers have the gift of a sense of smell like a wild forest creature's. Sleep is also an activity for tomorrow. The Germans are bold enough to think innovatively, avoiding clichés. They will understand me. Lucky for that. But what is luck? No fortress is impenetrable. Somehow, someone highly motivated always finds the key, the key to the problem.

The Prosecutor was questioning Ivan Ivanovich Ivanov, KGB colonel, a cripple, but not mentally, who was always attempting in any way he could to portray the Lithuanians as unsympathetic.

(Good reputation, plans for the future)

— Gentlemen, — says Jagger, rising to his feet. Acquiring the wild beasts' superiority over humans, learning to pick up smells from a kilometre away, remembering and recognising various scents, and, with the creation of certain coefficients, divining the indivinable. I had the honour of participating in the "50" seminar with representatives of fifty of the most wealthy families in the world. I can tell you that their ideas match ours in many ways, but the realisation of the Empire of Art will have to await a future time when we are able to demonstrate what rock performers can do. Nature is our teacher for solving any sort of problem. Incidentally, an amber pipe with a transmitter installed has been found. Ivan Ivanovich Ivanov or whatever his name is gave it to Mekas, and Mekas gave it to me. What a nerve — typical grandiose Russian effrontery. At the seminar I saw a documentary film about a biological weapon: bees in Brazil. The apiary is financed by Ivanov. So is a laboratory on the U.S. — Mexico border, and a laboratory staffed by a whole division of Mary the Snitch look-alikes. They work in the gene-hunting field, in Mexico. There's also a mind control laboratory there, which is doing research into the workings of the human brain. Total control is the aim; water with ionised colour markers is used, which sensors in the blood detect and thereby reveal which parts of the brain are being used, and how and when the ions are dashing around the vascular system, and what words your quivering tongue is formulating as it follows your thoughts, because the base of the human tongue vibrates according to what the person is thinking.

— Gentlemen, — said Bill Gates at this point, — I know lots of people who divide their life into two parts: life before Gates and life after finding out about Gates' philanthropic activities

Such things are always pleasant for me to know. I have bought a few KGB agents. I won't name them, I just wanted to make the point that money is

16

Communism, it's paradise, because you can buy everything. However the best gift is not a fish for the table, but a fishing rod, which enables someone to catch their own fish for the table. That fishing rod is Ringo Starr's Mental Technique. The way to be happy in any hierarchical situation. The mind has to work; the mind – making use of all the human spiritual treasures and trying to gain something for itself.

In fascist Germany there was a totalitarian 'security' apparatus, and in Stalin's Russia — the same. And in the future? Presumably criminal activity will die out in the future, because every person's mind will be controlled by technology, and all the water will have ionised colour markers in it, while above the city or region — radio waves will be bouncing around off radio towers.

That's what money can do. In Russia you don't even need to be literate to become a millionaire. The reptilian base of the brain still comes to the fore. The KGB works miracles. They also give other countries ideas. Only extensive funding of education can or will achieve results for humanity. However, such funding has to be under the supervision of media and religious bosses, as must the 'free thought' of the masses.

(Re: Being first among nations)
(Written by the Lithuanian.)

Jonas Mekas also made a speech:

— Lithuanians, who live on the doorstep of big countries, have become used to being careful. You never know who the terrorists are. I will take this opportunity to remind you that Lithuanians used to cut a hole in the German knight's belly, pull out his intestine and nail it to a post, and force him to go round and round the post winding his steaming intestines as he went ... Did we invite them? No. We defeated the Tartars and the Teutonic Knights. Lithuania extended from the Baltic Sea to the Black. The people who live there still think highly of the Lithuanians. That's what it means to have a good reputation. It comes centuries later. But it's there. Meanwhile, Russia ... — Jonas Mekas continued ... — The battle against lice is never pleasant, although it can be associated with secret pleasure ...

❊ ❊ ❊

(Written by the Spaniard.)

— Is that horrible enough for you? — Keith Richards asked the girl.

— Pretty horrible, — the girl replied, — but I'm still a long way from orgasm.

Campfire, hanged bodies, seven Russian heads, night.

17

Rolling Stones show in Prague

(Re: Good reputation)

Twilight frescos — a backdrop for Jonas Mekas' album, which has 111 people in it: relatives, schoolfellows, workmates, friends and chance acquaintances. Everybody has such an album, because once you have dealings with a person on more than thirty occasions, that person becomes a guest in your hotel of memories.

On the stadium screen: images from the rocker sect called Ringo Starr's Mental Technique; images that explain life and give us the understanding of how to be happy and how to relate to each other.

Musicians play, Jonas Mekas recites, in *hip hop* style.

(2. One of us, not one of us)

Memory monads — this is a memento that should never be far away, always close at hand. Our places, our people. Our way of life. A hotel that is always with you, with its inhabitants. We can find peace of mind and self-confidence only there where we feel at home and among our own kind.(11. The plan, correct or wrong)

Like it or not, a foreign country debases newcomers. And the quality of happiness falls. Exoticism and curiosity push people into making mistakes, because the true happiness of knowing — that is a theoretical labour by lamplight or a series of slowly progressing episodes that keep coming back like the blues, which we slowly adorn with timid observations.

Algis R. and Virgis B.

The three of us rented a bachelor flat in Partizanų Street. There's no rainbow without rain. It's true, they didn't say no to a shot of the hard stuff. Yes, their women keep getting prettier, and there were plenty of them. Indeed, they had their shortcomings, but in the end they were good friends, good sons, good fathers and, well, yes ... reasonably good husbands — category: from the rain clouds to the moss-blackened tree.

Now let's cautiously feed the world's rumours. Even with your eyes closed the group „Nuogi ant slenksčio" ["Naked on the Doorstep"] dazzles you. Algis sang with them for people like himself — hippies.

There certainly were pubs, and weddings, but no one stuck fivers on his forehead. His life on the stage was the most meaningful time of his life, which he remembers with poignant nostalgia, now that he is working in London.

There were trips to Yugoslavia with a bucket of nails, and jobs in Norway, because the family had to be supported. Bringing cars from Holland and

Germany ... On the stage he did not achieve as much as he would have liked to. What's that shining so strangely in the sky? It's the light of youth. The hotel that is always with us.

Re: a highway not far from Munich. Let's have sex. Not many cars passing.

The smell of ripe rye. Almost daily a local bourgeois homeowner rides by here on his horse. But only in summer.

Jagger, the bum, is experiencing real hunger. He picks a few lilac leaves and chews them. According to his calculations, if he can at least get a few drinks tonight he will manage to survive for another week.

His thoughts revolve constantly around Annette. How much does he have to lift his game so that she will fall in love with him? For the moment he feels humiliated and deprived. Jagger will never forget this highway.

This is where he adopted his strategy to overtake Paul in an ethical way. I will cause a scandal and make a fuss, he told himself. The knight of the stage is always seeking applause. I have to get him on the hook. Then there will be a struggle, a long struggle, until the fish is in the net.

I concentrate on the heavy breathing, which helps an exercising person get through the exercise. Somehow this dilapidated highway is beautiful to me. I am looking for the energy and the means to enjoy it to the fullest.

(5. Love, sympathy, friendship)

— You'll be sorry if you try to take me morally,- says Romutė. - Did you hear me?

— I heard you, — says Algis, — I'm at least a little interested ...

— Don't make me laugh, — says Romutė. — I should tell you to go to hell, but I like blue eyes, those little blue patches of heaven.

— I'll take the top off this baby, — says Algis holding up a bottle, — "Starka" is good vodka. I think the Etruscans invented it, those guys in the sarcophaguses in the shade of the cypress trees.

— That's a shock to me, — says Ramutė.

Algis accompanies the Etruscan theme and the "Starka" theme with an illegal smile.

— Good health, — says Ramutė, his wife, and they rub noses like two guard dogs in the yard.

There are many such scenes.

Algis, along with Strielčius, Atstovas, Kapralas, Aksomas, Mokasinas and Lėščius (he's now in USA) you once made Kaunas famous ... Jovial fat Džanis with the double chin, which had as many folds as a the Lord of the Manor's chin, he held you to be Lithuania's king of rock and roll.

19

(3. Hedonism)

You'll spend fifty just to find out whether the hornets — girlies — still come to your honey. And there you are on the stage. Not quite the same calibre as Mick Jagger, but an army, nonetheless.

(3. Hedonism)

The Gypsies applaud furiously, as if they had won the pie eating competition. A washed-out looking person, maybe from a committee, pays a fiver for a piece of happiness; the evening in the "Vakaras" continues. Son, what do you hope to do when you grow up, asks the man who proffers the fiver, Venzberg (202 cm), maybe a three metre high victory column? The kid looks a little worried. But you are too washed-out, too washed-out to test him; that's why people evolved from the cave-dweller stage, so that various thoughts could scratch around in their heads, culminating in putting their faith in "Starka" and in grandma's moonshine.

Meanwhile Mokasinas gets a smack from the Gypsy and rises silently, like a column of mercury.

The thread of bohemian moments winds from the dancing spool: forward!, cries Don Quixote, — adventures and banquets await us ...New York. Fifth Avenue. With a Police escort, Bill Gates demonstrates what hedonism is. He asks people this question and solves it.

The Armenian émigré is cooking kebabs while Gates and Jagger drink white Georgian wine (the type Stalin liked) and they have a bite of roast lamb.

In three hours they drank five bottles of wine each; they were merry, but they did not sway.

The next morning Bill Gates told journalists who came to meet them: — "Our heads are as clear as glass, no hangovers. Three cheers for Stalin's wine, three cheers for a little enjoyment, for tea and coffee, for little delicacies, the little pleasures of life.

(Good reputation; one of us, not one of us)

Hunched over your books you seek to find traces of a good reputation for humans, as scholars have sought in all centuries, keeping an eye on what the peer group is doing and how you should live. You want a lot from life: it would suffice to be yourself among your own friends, and to occasionally be a bit of a leader ... It's the autumn of your life. The park's ponds and paths are full of yellow leaves. But we can be glad that we were able to enjoy the company of a decent fellow, not a brat / no-hoper, who although he messed around a little still always managed to stay proper and likeable. That's all it takes. You can see the firm from afar. All the embellishments are unnecessary. Algis suits the beige

20

colours of sunset. Silver flecks in his hair, but we are still — back there, in our youth.

(*11. Plan, mistake-not mistake*)

On the other hand — Virgis, his character is to be quiet (although he had a talent for eloquent public speaking when required). In his youth Virgis wrote poetry in Russian *à la* Jesenin. A subtle fellow, always checking to what extent the theories of Kazanov, Baltazar Kosa and Ernest Hemingway are still practised today.

From age 10 to 33 we talked daily. Englishmen talk about the weather. We two talked about Janis Joplin, the Beatles, the Rolling Stones and the Doors. The pleasure we derived was almost sexual.

A month in Leningrad right after completing high school was the best month of my life. At that time I still thought I could become a Jean-Luc Goddard.

We had conversations about books and films in the inner courtyard of the Čiurlionis Gallery, not far from my place. Wherever he was, I was there too.

We discussed unsuccessful love affairs, which leave a bad taste in the mouth ... sitting silently on a bench, Virgis hiding is child-like sky-blue eyes (all the more noticeable because of his brown, not blonde, hair).

We were no saints. No one knows for sure whether it was Brutus that was the first to stab Julius Caesar, and you have got your hopes up for nothing if you were hoping to hear something happy about Virgis. I'll just let this observation slither down to the floor at your feet. One fine day, both smiling happily, both Virgis and I said farewell to each other with glances imbued with good rock and great chicks. All of that is as real and as tangible as a table or chair — a solid and material fact.

Mick Jagger approaches each girl with a plan worked out on the basis of other girls he has known before. The most important, of course, being Annette. This accent on love – it's special, and constant. Yes, there were nicer girls. Decency is one of Annette's characteristics. Perhaps in the top five.

Love is the world championship, coming from who you met along your life's path or read about, or saw on the screen. It is a serious and complicated task. Only afterwards do we arrive at the motif: love, major love or unrepeatable love.

(Author's voice, part Sorge, part Stirlitz...)

— It would be interesting to know how Paul McCartney or David Bowie or Sharon Stone pass their time. These days it's not hard to find out how the high-flyers live. You don't need a lot of money, my lovely, — I told the girl who kept betting on 13 on the roulette.

— You think the high-flyers are the happiest people around? — she asked.

You have to have a good job to be able to be happy in life. The oldest and most ingenious human invention, namely — money, it's a lift that takes you up to whatever hotel room you can afford. Yes, money is the lift that takes you to hotel-heaven or hotel-hell.

The question is: how to make money with the least hassle? Your job needs to coincide with your hobby.

Right from the start, money means communism. Since four thousand years ago.

The musicians were playing, a warm-up band. The audience (10,000 people) could feel that something meaningful was going on, and the name Ringo Starr's Mental Technique was warming their blood, as were the ideas being expounded by Jonas Mekas.

— Hotel, album, hotel again, the themes rolled around, — my computer spits out information about the 111 people close to me, and so it is for everyone. This is very carefully rounded off information using a method that has been appropriate from the time of the Sumerians right up until the Bush era. Virgis and Algis were both generals in the "One of us, not one of us" column, and lieutenants in the "Good reputation" column. They were seekers, maybe they lacked independent thought, they lived like the rest, imitating the man in the street, with occasional flashes of originality. In the "sympathy, friendship" column they were also lieutenants, but I respect that particular rank. By comparison, in the "Meals, clothes, sleep, transport" column they were sergeants. A spartan holiday camp was good enough for them. Their literary salon was a pub, and their communing with nature was done in public parks and along riverfronts. A few student girlfriends substituted for a fancy brothel, and as for love — well, only a few times in their lives. They like it. They're plain folk. Happy without emigrating, just staying in their own land, where the spirit of their parents, relatives, friends, and fellow travellers on the road of life hangs in the air like a morning fog. Their native land is their hotel — whether it be vagabonding and sleeping in the street (one star), or jail — or the highest category luxury hotel. As the Jewish insight has it: being happy with what is there.

In the "Meals, clothes, sleep, transport" column: I go to the forest by trolley bus. No Porsche is necessary. This is the only column where you need much money. Did Einstein, who hob-nobbed with royalty, have much money? I imitate him. The "Good reputation" column, and the "Being first in every competition" column — in these money does not help much either. Same for the "sympathy, friendship, love" column.

Charlie Watts and Rolling Stones show

(10. Good reputation)
(Written by the Lithuanian)

Why do we love our sense of smell? Because it helped us to give up smoking. No dog who smokes will have a good tracking nose. We should learn from nature.

Re: village, barking dog.

Let's have sex.

The acoustics are good, even though it's not a dip and the forest is not close. The barker is a baritone.

I have to go another 20 km, says Jagger to himself. I'll get to the railway station for sure, because I'm heading northeast. Yuck. I'm thinking about "Yesterday" and "Michel". What an inspiration, to compose those lyrics! Yuck. I would rather die than go on without finding a way to create such music.

Obliquely that dog served for something more than just making pups. As if by miracle, thanks to that dog I patented a golden ambition spring.

Paul, I'll give you a lift. And again the heavy breathing — a return to contemplative mode. From the side it looks like a friendly sparring match between partners. Spectacular!

The warm-up band is playing the Rolling Stones' best hits. Scenes on the screen are lending support to Watts' words.

— What I have discovered, — says Watts, — is a how to use the drumsticks with a laconic whack, but enough energy to hypnotise. When I started, no one played like that. Every song — just three or four smells. There are no bad smells. They are all good. Some soothe us, others give hope. Others are familiar. They are the aura of our ancestors. The experience of people who once were alive. We should be precise when we describe smells. Than are more smells than there are words to name them. Sometimes impossible to trace back through logical processes. Intuition is a more complicated process than logic. Going to the toilet is a creative process, because you are supplying life-giving nutrients to future plants and trees.

I will tell you how we write down motif and lyrics. If we were to write the words I just mentioned as notes, you would get a statement to which you would have to add a sentence containing drama and tragedy. Just for the heck of it, let's repeat the words "I will tell you how we write down motif and lyrics", but with sequence, i.e. higher. Now we need something that grabs you by the heartstrings: "My God, I'm dying, I can't fight back". That way we create a hundred songs and after having a rest we choose ten of them and then write the

23

lyrics, changing the melody a little. The guitar strums "I'm OK". With three voices we bung in "oh, what will I do?" and the instrumentation comes the same way: drama, lyricism, familiarity (or not) — typical, accustomed, a motif that is common in life. In creating the melody there is a development and dénouement of the idea, than a conclusion, and we glue it to the phrase, which could be a phrase composed of six bars, if they have enough freshness and drama. John Lennon hid jottings for musical motifs in the bathroom and kitchen. I record the intonations of ordinary people as they speak on radio and television. The most original intonations give birth to the nicest melodies.

A certain drummer, Vytenis Rožukas, a pupil of Europe's best drummer of the era, Vladimir Tarasov, created a new method of musical notation. The notes are indicated by numbers.

C — 1, C sharp — 2, D — 3 and so forth.

Length of notes: whole note (semibreve) — 0.1; half note (minim) — 0.2; quarter note (crotchet) — 0.3; etc.

Pauses: whole (semibreve) — 0.1; half (minim) — 0.2; quarter (crotchet) — 0.3; etc..

Name of notes.

C	C#	D	E	E #
1	2	3	4	5

Pauses _o__half__quarter_♪___
0.1 0.2 0.3 0.4 etc.

Major intonation +
Minor intonation –
Summary intonation ++

Symbols:
Tremolo ~
Accent /
Louder 1>, 2>, 3>
Crescendo >...
Diminuendo <...
Slow, quicker, very fast 1, 2, 3 ir etc.
Treble clef ↑
Bass clef ↓
Hold --------
Join ➔

The notes run across a computer screen, the score for the conductor — running ribbons on the screen with windows. There is a similar window for the musicians.

Example:

He patented that system of annotation as LATGA™ and perhaps once the attachment to the customary system of annotation is overcome, we will move on to annotation by numbers. This is what you see on the screen. Three notes are indicated as examples.

	1	2	3	4	5	6	7	8	9	10	11	12
	A	B	C	D	E	F	G	H	J	K	L	M
I												
II												
III												
IV												
V												
VI												
VII												
VIII												
IX												
X												
XI												
XII												
XIII												
XIV												
XV												
XVI												
	1	2	3	4	5	6	7	8	9	10	11	12
	A	B	C	D	E	F	G	H	J	K	L	M

The second octave is "si" bemol = c 4610=cIV10=cKIV10

That's just an outline for musical theorists. Just the beginning. I have been too lazy to work on perfecting this system; I appeal to you, maybe one of you will take it up. Giotto painted the circle, and I have found the dramatism of accent in the melodic subject. And my students coincidentally created a new musical notation system.

Acting x scenes
Counterpoint, accompaniment
Sequencing
Intonational subject with dramatism or several heroes.

10. Good reputation
(Written by the Englishman)

Mick Jagger comes to the microphone.

—Friends, he says, today I have something better to offer than playing my music. The money that you paid today you will get back, a hundredfold. I will set out for you the principles and practical philosophy of Ringo Starr's Mental Technique.

(1. Meals, clothes, sleep, transport
(2.)

These days we can get clothes from charity. Versace-modelled clothes for plebs like me? What's the use of that? You can get soup at Caritas [Catholic charity organisation]. Who needs it? I mean, for example, I like red caviar, and French wines and cheese—but what's the point of it?

Napoleon used to sleep for just five hours. I sleep more. One can sleep on the floor. Sleeping on cardboard on the pavement—that's the lowest level in this category. In other words, it's essential to have somewhere to sleep.

Transport. Walking 20 kilometres on corn-ridden feet, that's one star; flying Business Class and driving around in a Ferrari—that's three or four stars.

These days the only five-star things, in terms of transport, are hot air balloons or a 'break' ('*brička* ' — an open carriage with bench seats) drawn by five fine horses. Trolley buses, trams—these items are for sergeants.

For each rank—its own advantages and its own pleasures.

(3. One of us, not one of us)
(4.

You feel great when you are received warmly and you live the way your neighbours do, and the way your relatives and your peer group do. I sense the smell of an old person's house. That is a parabola that is seldom mentioned. Higher mathematics. In a thin jet the aura of the old man and lady goes to one's nose. What's it like? Maybe the taste of bogbean? As someone returning to my homeland, I sense it keenly. It's a smell left over from funerals. When you buy a house or flat, first you need to find out who lived there before.

If the "One of us, not one of us" item were to be resolved, the Arabs would no longer kill Christians and Sunnis would no longer kill Shi'ites. But at the moment the reality of the "One of us, not one of us" item is proved by the fact that Russians can't stand Chechens, and Chechens can't stand Russians; that's how grandfather's generation acted, that's how today's generation acts. The Oxford scholar plays tennis with one of his former fellow students and defines a circle "One of us, not one of us". This item is a question of standards, not free improvisation.

There is generation-to-generation transfer of bad examples, fighting, swindling. In the jails you have 'hawks' and 'bitches'; and in the army—old chums and new chums.

Most of these unfortunate patterns are repeated by each generation because they simply and uncritically adopt the attitudes handed down by the previous generation concerning "One of us, not one of us". The proof of this is the ongoing ill feeling between Jews and Germans, Arabs and Jews, Americans and Communists, Americans and Arabs.

These are great tragedies. Last week in Iraq more than a hundred people died. And all because of "One of us, not one of us".

People need to think independently, not just cling to stereotypes.

(Re: Jagger, 3. Hedonism)

Aha! Just what I wanted. The German girl has told me her name. It's Annette. She is a Siamese twin. She reminds me of a cherry tree full of light pink blossoms. Smells great, and very pleasant on the eye. She has an aura too that takes me back to the days of Anna from Saint Petersburg.

I think she is dedicated to live life as a beautiful doll, putting all her talent and energy into that. I swallowed the hook. I thirsted to get involved with this woman who had so ingeniously chosen her role; maybe she even had an ingenious philosophy, because to conquer a woman is to make all those around view her with awe and fall in love with her.

—Could I be a dove, pecking around at your feet and cooing? I asked.

—Any dove pecking around at my feet and cooing needs to have a green card: one million dollars. Because even though I don't have one yet, my child is already the most meaningful thing in my life, and I see a future for him: he has to be rich, beautiful, and have a high I.Q. Also, I have to be in love with his father. So you see, it's not easy to get such a green card. It's all or nothing.

—My I.Q. is one hundred and forty.

—OK then, I'll put a tick beside that in my little notebook. And the million, have you got that?

—Sure, I have it, I said. Now all you have to do is fall in love with me, and I—with you.

Here's an example. In this case I got love worth five stars, while I gave back at best three.

(Re: 4. Profession, hobby, sport, culture, tourism)

In this category the Beatles and I are Generals. I can assert forcefully that this has the smell of stables, of horses. My grandmother used to water the tomatoes with horse piss. It's the smell from somewhere like that. Here is a fragment of a person's life. The sad tsarina, the sage of my Hotel, will help you to derive some benefit from my album. Just be as patient as rain.

Who was first to go out, and who was second? Charlie; Charlie went out to have a leak. We had been partying in some sort of national park. Lucy and I, and my friends Charlie and Keith. She and her friend, also a diver, had been hitchhiking, just out of Liverpool. You know, that was the Woodstock era.

Questions and answers, we got along like a house on fire. The debates bubbled. The three of us raised such a commotion in the car, like a whole class of juniors getting on the tram.

We were met by the caretaker, who had a jaw that protruded like a shelf full of the works of Lenin. She had a pained expression as if her shoes were hurting and she started ranting about English hippies, so dissolute, such as Ireland had never seen, not even now, let alone in the days of her youth. Once that lady gets wound up, her mouth opens and shuts like a toilet door in a pub. Keith is as much at home in pubs as a frog in a swamp, so he knows British women quite well, like a blind man feeling a hand in the black dark. You had better go and lie down—Lucy told Keith. From what I know about face colours, you look like you're about to pass out. Marijuana and women, always new ones. We were as carefree as thistledown floating on the wind.

The pallid autumn watercolour put us in the mood for a high level relationship. She was a champion sportswoman, a high-diver, maybe even from the ten-metre tower; and maybe she even felt a flicker of love.

Lucy in the sky with diamonds. Youth hurtles forward, silently and meaningfully, like a symphony conducted by Herbert von Karajan.

Maybe she had just come off her period; maybe she was mad at her boyfriend or offended by his not giving her enough attention. A chain of coincidences, as a result of which—love after thirty minutes of becoming acquainted.

Life would be as black as the black paint on an artist's palette if there were no such adventure or no likelihood of them. Those adventures have the scent of heavy perfume, a capricious whiff of perfume. You shudder for a fraction of a second, then your energy sluice gates open. Like the first time you heard a cuckoo bird in the forest. Exotica is a little kitten with blue eyes.

(5. Love, sympathy, friendship)
(Written by the Spaniard.)

I know some people who only cultivate this category. At some stage I was one such enthusiast. And I'll be solicitous enough to tell you about it.

We were as agile and full of hope as swallows, diving around in the attic of the barn.

The girl from the Arklių Street dance hall.
***

Now Bill says to Mick:

28

I don't know your name, but I bet it sounds great compared to other words.

That girl is straight from a dream. A blue song. A face that is gentle and severe at the same time. Not even the hungriest shark would hurt her. Love rises in invisible steps of ether, but the soul is an anchor that weighs it down.

We are playing for a dance at Arklių Street dance hall. The Boss' name is Jack. He knew everything about music and about life, except for one thing: which girl is a gonorrhoea carrier, and which one is clean. These old guys have harder bones. More than one known troublemaker has felt the force of his hard fist.

Once I witnessed how a thug with an expression on his face as if he would readily strangle his own auntie for sixpence took a dive after getting whacked by Jack. He flew right across the dance hall and landed on his head.

I easily won her away from the rotter, who she might have found attractive if she liked a regular face and bushy eyebrows. The two of us sauntered along the street, gathering moonbeams. She had long legs like a pilgrim, and a long back like a sigh dying of thirst.

I think I only kissed her once as I ran for my train.

But the memory lingers on. Her smell—you'll excuse me, I'm not the best connoisseur of smells—was a little on the *Chanel* side.

The girl from the Arklių Street dance hall...

❀ ❀ ❀

—Are you terrified? Keith Richards asked the girl.

—Oh yes, said the girl, as she observed a cadaver climbing out of its coffin and sidling up to the fire to warm itself as it listened.

❀ ❀ ❀

(6. Family, children, parents)

—There is such beauty, recited Mick Jagger in a hip-hop way, before which words are impotent. The bar manager, who is as sweet as a bottle of vinegar, packed a hook to the head of a smartass from a London suburb. Order was restored. My half-brother James made an innocent side-step, like a temperance buff pouring out the contents of a glass onto a potted plant, and next thing a cross-eyed fellow crumpled up moaning; he was from the same London suburb. And in my genuine inebriation I chatted up his girl, who had a friend with her, and we happily passed the night together. In the morning a cup of *café au lait* and a woman's face, still fresh and gentle like a bunch of grapes.

When you look into it, every family's house or flat has a particular smell. Later on in life we miss it. How to describe it? We five rockers who have had nose jobs from a genial Swiss (may God admit him to Heaven), together with a material base of hundreds of millions, could quite seriously conquer such scourges of God as emigration, and likewise the Russian and Arab problems. My first memories of my father are of him washing socks, brushing his teeth, cooking potatoes, and other things along those lines. How sweet your dad's kiss is in your childhood. That comes from Freud, I think; or maybe Sophocles. Alas, I wouldn't want to discuss them with my other relatives.

One star. Modest.

(Re: 7. Catharsis)

—I am just a sinful fly, said Mick Jagger. You know, you can't force people to do things if they don't really want to.

She was wearing a beret, which was so weak and underdeveloped that it was as if it had been taken away too soon from its mother. Trachoma, rickets, tuberculosis?

It was ill, that beret.

But we got to know each other because of it, that beret.

For eight hours we drank whiskey and talked heart to heart. She talked to me; I cut her off and talked to her. When the ceiling began to revolve, we clung to our seats at the bar and drank on.

She drinks too much, she's too loose when dealing with men, and she's always dying her greying hair blonde. To tell the truth, I had a friend who, upon waking up after a big night of drinking used to go to a public toilet in the city so that he didn't suffocate his flatmates. That's the smell of this woman.

Here's a good example of catharsis. I'm not one to admire the gossipy manner of old bourgeois ladies. It seems too cheap to me.

But spontaneous sincerity—that's really something.

And another thing: the bath. At Haare the bathtub was separated from the shower by a high partition. Jagger was in the shower (the entry was in the corridor) and he heard that someone was in the bath. If it was Annette, he intended to climb over the partition and take her by force. That would be the beginning of my victory, thought Jagger.

He approached and looked. Yes, it was Annette lying in the bath.

—Mick, she said, on seeing his honourable face, I'm about to get in the shower, and I'd like to ravish you in there.

Jagger had second thoughts and told Annette: we need to be fiancées, we need to be courting for a year; only then can I sleep with a woman.

—You're more progressive than me. Don't look now; I'm getting out of the bath.

❀ ❀ ❀

(8. Beauty, fantasy, imagination, horror)

Keith Richards is playing flamenco. Campfire smoke.

—Through the flames I see a cried-out mother's face. Oh mother, do you hear the sounds of this autumn night from the dead? asked Keith Richards.

—Stop! said the girl. I think the most precious thing in life is a mother's heart.

The hanged men began to moan, moving their lips, which were meant for kissing children and grandchildren.

—They all go to the grave, all our dear ones, all 111 people in each of our personal albums, says Keith Richards to the accompaniment of Spanish music.

***

—People, Mick Jagger addresses the people in a Prague stadium. I have been making hay. When you hammer the blade of the scythe to even it out, the face of the hammerhead needs to be even, and you need a good steel block to put under the blade. And when you sharpen the blade, use a gentler file, so that you don't take too much metal off. Today I moved my cow to a new spot in the meadow, boy, was she happy! My cow gives twenty litres of milk; I'll have to get some fodder for her.

Eternity was born in rural areas, in the country. But actually, there are not that many rural smells. Only about five hundred. I'm trying hard to remember them all. That's my link to nature. The same bond that a mother cat has to her kittens.

***

The stadium is a turmoil of whistling and shouting.

Mick's fantasy is a winner.

***

— I'm not a plebeian, — says Bill Gates. — I'm guided by the Saint-Exupéry system: "Love is the flower that you water, having chosen it from among the others, without looking for a better one, you just water it, that's where the value is".

That's my finish in the Love contest.

(9. Winning in all situations, prestige in the group, prestige in society)

As he picked up cigarette butts at Fiumicino Airport, Mick recalled how he had done that at Haare. There in the smoking room his heart was beating like a skylark's heart, because Annette was keeping her distance and being sweet to Paul, not to him. Lighting a cigarette for her, Mick suggested they take a walk down to the pond, where two families of ducks lived.

31

—I would like to get to know you, to talk; I have to know for sure that my love is not blind, that you truly are my chosen one, that you're the best woman I have ever known.

But Annette, maybe because she did not trust herself, did not open her heart to Mick. She believed there were truly more talented and more beautiful women than her. She told herself: I'll let Mick keep the impression that he has of me.

Women. Nicaraguan princess. Human Heart No. 40.

What am I like now? I feel sexual pleasure when I demonstrate that there's nobody better than me within a 100-metre radius. Does that satisfy me?

What am I like now?

Slow steps of incorporeal shadows. Ghosts from the past. A blind chicken, because the rooster got his trousers torn on a hawthorn.

The two of us are drinking Calvados. Time came for her to depart. I was such a pig, I didn't drive her. Keith drove her. He came back three hours later. He was boasting that he didn't need any more women that night, he had already had one. I drew the logical conclusion, and from there it was downhill all the way until we split up.

Her body was an aquarium, and my eyes were piranhas. She had stretched a tendon and had her leg in plaster, but we never stopped making love. Her sense of humour would melt the hardest material. Get ready, old fellow, in a minute you're going to laugh. I remember how I was determined to make love with her in an airplane. Somehow I had missed out on that experience up until then. How silly I was.

She would never come to my place until lured by marzipan or a piece of cake. She knew how to charm with her crooked smile the fine group of people assembled in her living room, people you wouldn't meet in just any old café, or among what one might call 'ordinary people'.

For assiduously winning in all situations—she was a General. The scent of the first violet of spring.

(10. Good reputation)

—There's a blue glow, says Mick, leaning back on the ice of the pond. Bye, take care...

The taste of stage sweat in the mouth. Unforgettable. A lifetime on the stage. From the balcony of my old age I see my life. Yes. It was nice. To me it's the smell of freshly mown grass, especially if the grass was a little dry. Like hay. That's all. And I'm grateful for that. Very much so. Sometimes, in spring, the smell of slushy melting snow. That's all.

Uncle Vilnius. Trackwalker. Human Heart No. 98. A strong smile, glued on. His monocle seems to look at everything mockingly. He is wise, that's all.

He has seen a lot and heard a lot, and he has made sense of what he has seen and heard.

He's like a dream that you dream within a dream.

He lived like he was in the barracks, with a sense of duty. A General in the Good Reputation category. Uncle Vilnius. Trackwalker.

(11. A plan, a correct plan; a mistake, no mistake)
(Written by the Spaniard.)

—The city is burning, Bill Gates informs us, shots are ringing out, but two chess players are continuing their game, mesmerised by enthusiasm. That's probably how it was. May be what happened. Maybe. Anything is possible.

Your correspondent, talented but ruined, acknowledges: in life a plan is the most important thing. A concert pianist who each morning goes over the notes in his thoughts for a few hours—a few hours! That's a daily checking of each day's plan; it's a chess game, in which all our talents, all our education and all our experience come into play.

Good and exact standards—these are the guarantees of success on the path of life.

Unconditional adherence to certain moral standards (as in Catholicism, Islam, Judaism, Buddhism) facilitates and simplifies the struggle for the quality of happiness in any of the 11 points on Ringo Starr's periodic table.

The human race has been on this planet only a few minutes, but it has about eighty years to go. Our civilisation is fragile and naïve. And very young.

Let's establish research laboratories that can put names in the empty spaces on the world map.

Politics, art, media—these are dad's straps, which kiddies need. What sort of morality, conscience, principles do kids have? The human race is just a big kindergarten.

Be tolerant.

Carefree planning of each day—this is the root of all tragedy. The wayward human race resists the discipline of wisdom. Hubris is a disease for which the human race foregoes fully-fledged happiness.

I'm like that, I'm guilty.

A middling student goes on to give a middling performance in life. I.Q. is already noticeable at school.

What would Alexander the Great do in my place? He would involve 10,000 people in his activities, and with their smells and their auras he would leave a significant mark in world history.

Tomorrow I will talk on BBC television.

In my codex of honour, I won't hide it; my ideal is Alexander of Macedon. Here are 10,000 of you and I am your leader, I improve your standard of life; I am strong, I have more than one hundred million dollars, and being strong I help

33

the weak, thereby winning the hearts of millions of people, their love and, above all, their respect. My team consists of Paul McCartney, Ringo Starr, Keith Richards, Charlie Watts, Annette Hess, Sean Lennon and Jonas Mekas. Also Rod Stewart, David Bowie and Cat Stevens. With this team of 'noses', and in general a team of geniuses, we will achieve more than Alexander the Great.

Crookery? What for? It's not as if there is no legal path.

The hedgehog. I wonder how they have sex?

My heart is full of love for this hostel, this student residence that is our world, with all its people, urbanists, nature and animals. I idealise the hotel we call Earth, I idealise all its inhabitants. And in idealising them I love them purely. That is God-like logic. In the jungle the law of the jungle prevails, but in our civilisation—God-like logic. That's as much as has been achieved up to now.

A bad plan, lack of training, lack of I.Q. We should open our hearts to the poor without expecting thanks. That is God-like logic.

In the dictation test of life, those who are looked up to by most of the world's people should be the ones to correct the mistakes. We, the old rockers, are the gurus of our generation. Our project maximum would be establishment of an Empire of Art; our project minimum would be getting at least two people to believe in our teachings about Arabs, Russians and immigrants—then we could call our project a success when we knocked on the Pearly Gates to be admitted by Saint Peter. What is that smell? That is the smell of a nightingale in full-throated song, singing on the bushy banks of a lovely river, where the waves lap at the shore and give off a smell of boat lubricants and mud.

Hemingway's romanticism about exotic countries—that was a mistake with big consequences. It smells of diarrhoea, cholera and withering flowers. Brrr... Creating a correct ideology is as hard as designing and building an aircraft or a space ship.

At the moment I am making a montage, choosing from life whatever is most meaningful, old, tried and true, folkloric – womanly and ingenious – manly.

The point at which things become standard has been checked; likewise a new discovery, which later becomes standard.

It's the feeling of an infant suckling at the breast. After that he prattles and chirps, waiting to hear a horror story. It's OK, mum is right here.

Yes, we old rockers are right by.

The Czech woman Natasha, and the Slovak Jana—they are nearby and they love us, and we love them. And not just because Slavic women are the best, and British lads the finest (as a British literary figure wrote). Bill Gates has just one ideal. Achilles. Alexander the Great was Achilles' pupil. Whereas Achilles' teacher was the compact energy of the nightingale, its fullness and rounded sharpness.

34

In the high-rise building in the centre of Haare there was a coffee machine on the bottom floor. Annette used to drink coffee there and gossip.

She used to find something to chat about with Paul, but she kind of didn't notice Mick.

One time Mick, overcome with anger, threw away his untouched *cappuccino* and went to chat up a certain black woman, who was a patient on the seventh floor of Haare hospital.

—I've had a yellow woman, and a white woman, but I haven't had a black woman.

Hurt, Annette said that the black woman was a tramp, who gave herself to anyone. Jagger retorted:

—I've had an English woman, an American woman, a Nicaraguan woman, but not a German woman.

—Well lucky you, said Paul. It's all still in the future for you.

❀❀❀

The Russian-speaking Grim Reaper moves its jaws; Keith Richards pours the girl some tea. The hanged men swing on the creaking gallows, and the ghost in the coffin nods its head.

—No one applauds a singer when he gargles, said Keith.

—Well I think, said the horror-seeking girl, he is not one of the narrow specialists (this species died out, only the universalists are left). Mick Jagger— universal genius.

❀❀❀

(Written by the Englishman.)

—Tell me, Mick Jagger said into the microphone, which musicians have sold the most tickets?

—The Rolling Stones! shouted the audience.

—Yes. But every person is a speck of dung. Don't adopt positions that make that apparent. Our shows—they are Keith Richards' hymn to Rhythm 'n' Blues, which has deep traditions. Can we expect a little advance?

—Yes, boomed the stadium.

—Let's honour Jonas Mekas, John Lennon's friend. He likes to say "As the ancient Lithuanians used to do..." To paraphrase, I would say: "As our old rockers used to do...", love, are you making love?

—Yes!

—Love, freedom and flowers. No to war!

The stadium erupted in ovations.

—Now you see where the roots of our ideology are. It is the smell of semen, the smell of crushed poppies sobbing, one of Christ's smells. Plain, strong, dependable. When all is said and done, it is the smell from an excited woman's mouth. I could choose Miss Universe with my nose. John Kennedy is no more, but Jagger still sings for you. From time to time the Lithuanians splash the tree of freedom with their blood. A proud but not numerous nation, they are like a moose stalked by wolves. Jonas Mekas will attest to that. His creative output is good, like a Finnish knife. It is *fluxus* art, a sharp wave crest in the ocean of banal information. Hippie love—that was playing for a bigger prize than sex. We should all love one another. That is a precise and reliable plan.

Jonas Mekas comes up to the microphone.

—What's up?

—Be careful, the Mongols and Tartars are attacking, he says. The Slavic Mongols are spreading through the world like piranhas. In my life I have seen a lot of Russians, and they were all nationalists. I believe that the hanging gardens of Jagger's music will bring those stinkers back into the human fold. It's not much I want, all I ask is that the Russian stinkers stop stinking. Nationalism—that's flypaper. How many flies run the risk of getting stuck to it? We have quite a lot of nationalist flies. Lithuania's nationalists—they are piggies who dream to fly.

—And what are the Rolling Stones? asked Jonas Mekas. They are like a particularly enchanting woman, who was understood and studied as the model for the Rolling Stones style.

The stadium is awash with shouts, catcalls, and whistles. The Ringo Starr's Mental Technique sect leaders are fraternising with their followers. It's just as much fun as when the Rolling Stones played Rock and Roll for their fans.

❁ ❁ ❁

—Nothing of the sort! the Lithuanian writer retorted to the Russian writer, who was frantically trying to dominate, muttering the phrase that has been the mantra of the Russians since 1941: You Lithuanians are fascists, you shot us in the back.

The "Europa 2000 Literary Express" was stopping in Paris. The town was full of poets and translators. Poems were being read, that had been translated during the trip from Lisbon. Each nationality group had people who could translate into English, German, and Polish. Relations between the groups were warm and pleasant. Except that the Russians and Lithuanians clashed and clearly did not like each other. In the smoking lounge of the train discussions ensued.

—I think we need to include Robert Plant, said the Russian. His fine *"Immigrant Song"*...

—The lots were drawn fairly, said the Lithuanian. If you had your way, the film novel would be about the 'savage' Chechens, with which the Russians are never going to make peace.

—You have no talent. Were there metaphors? No? asked the Russian. No, there weren't. Were there images, characters? No, there weren't.

36

—In a film novel, says the Englishman, images are not necessary. The character is in the actors, in their nuances of relating to each other. There are twenty types of person. Actors are a montage of those twenty types.

—I will portray a KGB man in relation to the first item: food, clothes, sleep, household chores and transport, said the Russian. These are very real brush strokes. In our horror thriller realistic details are vitally needed—like air.

—I would like to make a suggestion, says the Pole, and you know that more than one Pole has been awarded the Nobel Prize, so you should take my suggestion very seriously. We need to order a wreath for the "Top 50" group of billionaires all over the world. Democracy and the free market are the political project of these times. It's a workbench, onto which are squeezed the middle class and the lower class. It's a historical process. A universal, unified, evenly integrated world economy is exactly what globalisation is not. For most people, the prices of merchandise in the market are just the start of globalisation. And they depend not just on local or national prices, but on prices that are set in the global markets. In the past globalisation took place together with revolutionary movements and big wars. The same awaits us in the future.

—The World Bank, the World Trade Organisation, says the follower of Bill Gates, the International Monetary Fund and the Organisation for Economic Cooperation and Development, their aim aids the Great Transformation, which will bring on world civilisation. The last régime of the Enlightenment is the USA.

—I have already written my version of the novel, says the Englishman, but I am concerned about the prestige of the whole novel, and about what will be written later. Not one European country, except maybe Norway or Denmark, will be able to reconstruct a welfare state that could be associated with Social-Christian democracy.

—John Naisbitt said: "We are moving towards a world of 1000 countries. Countries are breaking into smaller, more effective units." A Lithuanian's voice in all this is like a horsefly's in a large zoo. What will the "Top 50" say? There are differences among the various economies. That's why global markets are thriving. Big profits are being made from exploiting the differences.

—Only the Jews know, says the Jewish writer with a yarmulke on his head, only we know that human capital is—migration. The USA is a dynamic and energetic country that has opened its doors to most of the world's poor. A compromise is necessary; people shouldn't have to give up their freedom in exchange for security. The winner takes all. The distance from bottom to top is enormous. I don't think we should adopt the many-times bankrupt idea of imposing our will and values, as the USA and Russia do. You see, democracy and the free market—they are not partners, but competitors.

—Gentlemen, the Russian says, cleaning his pipe, being first, that's what makes progress, and it's the correct style. Should the powerful be equal to the weak? All principled people with morals are fundamentalists. They are not career-obsessed. They believe their own ideals. In the struggle for morality and

37

values, Christians, Muslims and Jews should unite. They should not be hostile to each other.

—You know, the German interjected, North America was financed by the Rothschilds through their agent August Belmont, and South America by the Rothschilds' relatives, the Erlanger. Financial people are not politicians, and not ideological activists—they are hungry for power and honour, they are greedy and amoral people. Their enemies are those who do not belong to their circle. That's what the "Top 50" is about. They know that monopolies cannot be put in place without government help, and that is a network controlled by a tight-knit clique. No intellectual acrobatics required. Just arithmetic, that's all. In another 50 years Germany will dominate the world, because it is bold, capable and hard-working. It's too easy to go to war. There are a hundred other ways to achieve the result.

—I am melting from pleasure, the German Jew hit back, it seems one calls that National Socialism?

—Now, now, says the Russian. A chess battle is not a swordfight. Let's be gentlemanly. The information war is taking place first in the media, then in art. Military decisions are being taken in that quarter. This film novel is a force for national and international security.

*****

(Written by the Russian)

Ivan Ivanovich Ivanov

Smell of an attic where a cat lives. Acrid, energetic. The smell of a wolf tearing into carrion. Oh yes. *Davai, davai* [Russian for 'come on, come on'] here comes the barefoot angel, Ivan Ivanovich Ivanov, trampling the old lady's scarf that is called Lithuania, full of vindictive rage, wanting to put the Lithuanians 'in their place' with their Freedom Avenue of Kaunas, and the Seimas (Parliament) building in Vilnius, to squash them like ants out of their packed trolley-buses, to smash the asphalt into smithereens, and the Gediminas Castle of Vilnius too. They would bring in rationing, including sex rationing for all of Lithuania, for those sycophants and 'squealers', vagabonds, jailbirds (may they stay prisoners for all time), and the students—who are three times less bright than Muscovites, who can only yelp at the feet of Russian intellectuals. At this point Ivan Ivanovich meditates, because he has been in Italy, in that mafioso-ridden dump, Russian laboratory No. X. There's lots of Russians around the world, because we are rich, we have natural gas, petroleum, metals, uranium; because money is the most ingenious and widely tested invention. It's a lift up to communism, and we Russians aren't stingy with money for our laboratories, which are headed by the most talented people in the world. That's

38

why a Russian education is ten times stronger than any education you could get in any Spanish institution, let alone Oxford and Cambridge. Russia is a warrior nation, this era's Sparta, having taken everything good that the Mongols and Tartars had to offer (except for learning the Mongolian language). We defeated Hitler, we defeated Napoleon, and we were smart enough to create the Soviet Union. Any kudos it earned was due to the small nations in it, but all the honour went to the Russians; the Army, Posts and Telegraphs, polyclinics, hospitals—everything was in our hands in the territory of the Soviet Union. Yes, we'll put those mongrels in their place, in their place; the pitcher will carry water until it breaks. The European Union—I already see the signs of its disintegration. Discipline and careful planning—all that is on Russia's side, traffic regulations—laws—all on the side of Russia's tough government. We will triumph when we find a weapon that makes USA and Europe bare their bums to us. We are the creators of science, of the narrowest ideology, that's us! Happenstance will determine whether we turn out to be saints or murderers and whether the USA and Europe negotiate with us, because they are afraid, and we are intrepid. That running sore of Russian immigrants in the Baltic republics and elsewhere—it should be just a little nuisance for us and a scandal for them, not able to be swept under the rug, because that's how the Estonians, Latvians and Lithuanians see it. And Immanuel Kant, Adolf Hitler, Vladimir Lenin, Jack Nicholson, Barbara Streisand and William Shakespeare, all of whom were born at Easter, are just underlings, 'мальчики на побегушки' as the Russians say. The Russian temperament and I.Q. are quite fitted for making and implementing a plan, for dominating the world, oh yes, it's quite feasible for us to do it. Russia is a nightingale, a force and a fullness, enriched uranium hexafluoride, converted into uranium oxide powder, kept in special tubes, used for the production of nuclear fuel rods, with the reactor in a sarcophagus. The nucleus of the U-235 atom splits, releasing heat energy, which is used to generate electricity, but those nuclear weapons are child's play, we have thought up much more horrible things now ...

❀ ❀ ❀

(Written by the Spaniard.)

—Well now, asks Keith Richards, horrible?
—Oh yes, the girl replies, keep going.
Hanged men, campfire, a Russian-speaking Grim Reaper.

❀ ❀ ❀

(Written by the Russian.)

As I was saying, we have thought up much more horrible things now, with the help of non-government organisations, namely, fighting using the KGB like a stab in the emptiness. You see, a non-government organisation, private, secret,

39

already has an advantage against the advancing barefoot angels. We are armed, they are not. This is our power, almost fascism, maybe beyond fascism, think about it; but seriously, like you would consider jumping off a very high cliff. Proceeding this way we can ride the atomic juggernaut. Total control of mankind, ceiling computers relaying your thoughts to Central Office; town water supply and food products in shops—dyed. Let's see your chin, *davai, davai*. Plus a lot of Russian drunkards' swearwords (aren't we the leaders in this field?), — *Davai, davai*,—. The greater the treachery the more impressive it is, you 'stukach' ('squealer'), cough up more often, I'll give you a dollar fifty, if need be even half a million dollars. Ivan Ivanovich Ivanov draws an idea out of his duffle bag, he draws chaos out of an accordion's waves, he draws a distinction between the different types of trees in the forest, he draws something out of the ingenious ideology that forms the reader's, the audience's opinion about Russian science. He draws something out of real hardship, with laughable tragicomic hunger for praise; with yours, with his folk habits and standards, with a cobra-like reaction and a man-eating tiger's eyes. I launch my little boat in the Volga, for myself, for my family, for my nation, for mankind. I denounce Hemingway—that romantic fraudster? Talent, energy, beauty, I.Q.—all ours. For us, other nations are shark bait. About one third of the human race is like that. Russians are romantic heroes, like highflying pilots. Russians are Order and Mister Job Done, domination and sex, third world war code. The rest of you are just eating crumbs from the table of our science. A Russian is always young, never a victim of paedophilia on the banks of the Volga, silver, not your Californian cupro-nickel. I will throw you in the river and pull you out and fuck you, the spirit of Caligula and Tahitian cannibals is alive. Russia is reclaimed chaos, look for a new light bulb, our newborn are worthy of a museum, impressionist winters, abstract processes of the Russian soul. How much material, form and ideas have died, and not always with justification? Self-preservation—*se conservare*—is the purpose of all civilisations, because standards in the banal past—gold treasure, just clean off the dust and it will shine—I make bold to generalise that these are approximate truths, not exact, with many exceptions. That is Russia. (Are you bored?) For a Russian, the allure of battle is linked to a glass of vodka. The Russian race is undiluted genetic information from the time of the dinosaurs; your superficial Oxford graduate is incapable of understanding that. Contrast theory, tsar and Rasputin, complex—simple, that is the Russian spirit, and Ivan Ivanovich Ivanov is a major part of that plan, crippled, but not mentally, the finest pun of chaos, whose duty it is to put the baddie in his place.

❊ ❊ ❊

(Written by the Spaniard.)
—I want to too, I want to too, says the girl to Keith Richards.
—What do you want?

—To put the baddies in their place. Those that have crawled out of their coffins had better be afraid. ...

A campfire, gallows, a Russian-speaking Grim Reaper.

❀ ❀ ❀

(Written by the Russian.)

To put the baddie in his place, information, news, desires, ways of making your mark, customs, cleverness, belief that you are tough, fascination with conflict—these are Ivan Ivanovich Ivanov's subjects. One's heart rends to see the *prana* journey, sun, air, water, colours, 30 barriers separating even very good friends from each other, not to mention Jews from Germans, Lithuanians from Russians, Arabs from Americans, 30 barriers even in the best instance. Do we have to slit each other's throats over it? Emigration is a particularly cruel confrontation, with victims. Ivan Ivanovich Ivanov shits under the water in a Californian swimming pool, knowing that the sky of his homeland is the most important thing in life. But look how many people are silly enough to leave it behind! Really, without exception, money does not lead to happiness; money is communism, it just needs a wise dad's strap. We can politely walk away from anything that's dirty, but who will we fraternise with? Do we adopt a phlegmatic BBC dignity with a bullet-proof vice, do we adjust our code of honour? A Russian asks a Russian: Mistake—or not? The bourgeoisie and their standard defences. A Lithuanian will never sign a news item, because only ten out of every hundred thoughts become meaningful. A Lithuanian feels the way ahead with his stick, whereas a Russian rushes head first, chest out into the enemy line of fire to attack their bunker. A Russian belongs to that part of the human race who, like bohemians, blindly imitate the upper classes' nonchalance, you know—he's so tough that he thinks nothing of pouring a glass of vodka down his throat, his health is good, don't waste your time trying to convince him that Elton John didn't do Kirkorov (or was it vice versa?) Yes, there was socialism, which gave you free shoes that never fitted well, and today we seek another ideology and unique religion, one that gives us ozone (or *prana*). As for the Germans, let me tell you that they are brave enough to think independently, avoiding stereotypes. They are one of a kind—*sui generis.* So let's not put obstacles in the path of our being like that, let's pay more attention in our lives to battle systems: 1) pressure, 2) striking like lightning at the contour lights on the enemy craft, or else trying to get the high jump record, 3) avoiding conflict, and 4) knowing that there are no unexchangeable fortresses. AS our thoughts slide about in the slalom of UTILITY, the situation improves and the Russian's face (not his heart) says: but you could have done without all this—what do we tell him?—Envy, son, envy is the cause of brother murdering brother. Give you an excuse and you might do it, maybe saying that the fatherland is above kinship.

41

There are many reasons, they are various, but however it is, all is well. Fill your glass with the philosophy of the Jew being led away to be shot: that however it is, all is well. The sons of the East, the sons of the West, they all love those remarkable cliffs of the Volga valley. Be with me always, Volga, pure essence of the Lord. I love the Volga naturally, as I love the day and night. It's enough to travel a little on it to understand what inspires the Russian women. I suspiciously pricked up my ears, like a piano tuner, when I dreamed that this instrument was hurtling its way toward the abyss, tinkling as it went. But what about the awakened child's purity? Among six billion, my version is one of the more interesting: fantasy, beauty, romanticism, imagination, nonchalance. Maupassant–Lieutenant General; Stendhal–Major-General; Homer–Generalisimo. Nature is still more sensible than people, although if we are talking about colonies and Rock, it's true, the English are first. But a thousand laboratories are needed, of which maybe one will find a fragment of the true path. I believe in the laboratory idea, that's the path to improvement, the golden point of my condition. By the way, hedonism and desire to lead have accompanied us from ape-man times. So, even better, eat herring like a Jew and then every note of your thoughts will be professional. Don't forget that thirst for honour and fortune are not neighbours, the supply for the wisdom systems market is huge, and when the Eiffel Tower is moved to Džomolungma, a Russian will climb up on it and make a speech, which will put the truth more precisely. Once I was walking with a German. He said, wait a minute, hold my belt, and he had a shit at a suburban bus stop. That's the way to behave: an adequate catharsis.

The bittersweet faecal smell of that *enfant terrible* Adolph Hitler

(10. Good reputation)
(Written by the German.)

In Haare a certain cellist was chasing a very nice girl, who was maybe even nicer than Annette.

One day as a group was drinking coffee in the hall, Annette saw the beautiful lass approaching their group. Not wanting to compete in a situation where she might come off second best, Annette excused herself and went to the Empire of Art Contact Centre.

—You can take the girl out of the country, but you can't take the country out of the girl, said the beauty, imitating Annette's way of walking, but without clarifying what she was talking about.

Annette

(Written by the German.)

Max Schmeling, World Heavyweight Boxing Champion in the Hitler era, was 100 kg of wind-tanned body and a willingness to jump into the sea waves if it would earn him a drink of Schnapps. His fine, much-broken boxer's nose, he carried many years; likewise his head, which was quite unsuited for concentrated thinking.

There are many people at the graveside. Aged 99, Max Schmeling died as he lived.

In his time he had dined with Himmler, Governor-General Frank, and also with Goering. This was an honourable funeral costing about two thousand euros for one of Germany's most famous sportsmen of the past, one who had hob-nobbed with Generals. His big forehead, full of thoughts, his thoughtful profile. Hairy as someone from the Planet of the Apes.

—Friends, said Jonas Mekas at the graveside (the whole group was at the funeral, because this was what Annette wanted), this Lithuanian American, Jurgis Šarkis-Žukauskas, took away the World Heavyweight Boxing Champion title from our beloved Max Schmeling. Lithuanians knew Max well, but someone always comes along to defeat you. Strictly speaking, looking down from on high like the Lithuanian deity Perkūnas, today both Šarkis and Schmeling are in a similar position. But Max Schmeling reached such a venerable age, one that no sportsman, let alone a boxer, had ever reached. That's why no boxer, not even Joe Louis or Cassius Clay, has such an honourable reputation as Max Schmeling. Ninety-nine years for a boxer — a super achievement, who knows whether it will ever be surpassed? This German, World Heavyweight Boxing Champion, has his name written in letters of gold in the world history of sport. That's a real Aryan, fantastic breeding, which speaks for itself.

Annette, like an ancient portrait of beauty, stepped forward; the rain stopped, the wind eased, and the weather sobered up as if following the Minnesota Program.

—Friends, said Annette, don't be bitter; let your thoughts change course, like a kitten that feels the time has come to jump off your lap. How many of us are left? Us, the German heroes? Max Schmeling's sports career, his pedagogical career—he trained the Wermacht's most talented—coincides with the glory of German history. Yes, we have made mistakes, believing that we

43

were the strongest, the most capable, and the bravest. We are Germans; our arms end in intellectual scissorhands (Mick Jagger and Charlie Watts smile and nod their heads), and these have a tendency to lead us into victory. With a voice as intimate as a bird's heart I invite you to do everything to help protect these nest eaglets in Germany.

—Friends, said one of Max Schmeling's kin, clad in a raincoat, Max has made his will and in it he leaves all his wealth, 200 hundred billion, to Annette Hess, as the only trustworthy representative of the German Volk. He leaves it to her as a writer and a public activist, chosen by Nature itself to lead the National Socialist Party.

He went up to Annette, put a platinum ring with diamonds on her finger and kissed it.

—I am one of those who have been created for exceptions, not for rules, said Annette. I will try to quickly turn the page on the aura of the National Socialist Party, and I believe that the time will come when in the betting shops of the world the odds for the Germans will be 12 to 1 against the Germans and the Russians.

—In the projection of parapsychological space, says Mick Jagger, my God is the Rolling Stones, or Perkūnas, the ancient Lithuanian deity. He strikes the land with lightning and as a critic he is severe, but just. It takes courage to believe in him. *Themis*, holding the loaded scales of many a person, gets a Sergeant–General rating on the eleven-point scale. That's Perkūnas' bookkeeping report, the only path to truth, trampling on romanticism, searching only for true denominators, unafraid of criticism. And with thundering rolling stones, Perkūnas speaks: pagan religions are not a silly outlook on life. If we look into the banal values of the past, we find some ingenious forgotten ideas. For example, as a member of the Rolling Stones, I believe in the god Perkūnas, who is the god of rolling stones. Together with Pan, the Sergeant of Life, he determines my world view. Thanks to a special nose operation I am closer to Pan than anyone else. The intuition of a deer helps me to get oriented in the impotence of a rigid logical system. Paul McCartney and I are prepared to found the Empire of Art. Paul's and Annette Hess' and Bill Gates' billions would be enough to found such a country. We have an offer to do it in Raushen, a resort in Svetlogorsk, where Goering had a villa. We have three candidates: Druskininkai, Raushen – Svetlogorsk and Yalta, the place where the world was carved up. You ask us why we are so tough. We are from the rock world, the last revolutionary nucleus. We have more worshippers than John Kennedy, and more money too. Rudolph Hess, although he fell in with a crowd of baddies, left behind the best reputation in bygone Germany, and therefore it is entirely just and appropriate that Annette Hess has been chosen—as a representative of a super breed—to take a leading role at the funeral of the best World Heavyweight Boxing Champion of all time, Max Schmeling.

After the funeral Paul, Mick, Jonas and Charlie were travelling in the jeep with Annette. Annette, World Heavyweight Dumb-dumb Champion, quietly held Paul's hand as they drove along. Words are bees, but silence is honey.

44

Mick sat on the other side of Annette. He decided to hold her other hand. Annette smiled happily—one of the richest people in the world. She knew what the rockers were saying in their various spheres of activity. Greed, that shit-carter's hanky, climbed ominously behind like the forthcoming world flood. Jagger hated McCartney, and McCartney hated Jagger. But they had known each other too long and were too involved with each other. Peace will no doubt be restored, although feelings, like insects, crawl all over them, to this minute.

When he wanted to tease Annette, Jagger would refer to the black woman as "my slave from Nigeria" when the names were called for the guests to go up to the 7th floor restaurant at Haare.

Annette ran out of patience and saw to it that the black woman was transferred to a different building not far away.

❀ ❀ ❀

Re: Italy

THOSE IMMIGRANTS, SUCH PIGS

(1. Meals, clothes, sleep, transport, domestic requirements)
(Written by the Pole)

—Steal me a bicycle from the Olympic Village, said Annette, no doubt making fun of Mick Jagger.

Mick waited for someone to enter the high-rise building, which housed Eastern European athletes during the Munich Olympics (now—regular apartments). He went up to the 4th floor and somehow removed a nice new bicycle from a balcony. It was he, not Annette, who took the risk. Annette just giggled in the background.

—How are you? she asked him over the telephone.

—Two black eyes, and a dagger in the back, like 'Lemonade Joe' (*'Limonádový Joe'*, a character in a Czech surrealist film from 1964). Annette, I beg you, have pity on this poor lad.

—I am doing all I can to help you solve the problems of emigration, replied Annette, a cold look on her face.

Florence. Jagger and Watts haven't had a drink of water for two days. They keep asking for a glass of water in the railway station bars (there are three of them), but the Italian *ragazzi* won't give them any. That is their mentality.

They walked around for a couple of kilometres, but could not get anything to eat. Where's Caritas? You can't ask anyone in English.

With his hand Jagger churlishly grabbed a grape from a fruit vendor and ate it. The only food he had had for several days.

Back to Rome by train. No ticket-checker.

Where to sleep?   Jagger and Watts didn't want to sleep on cardboard, because they were worried about their bladders. But sitting all night outside Termini station gets boring, so they went for walks for about 3 – 4 blocks around the station. At night the interior of the station is locked and inaccessible. Near the door, on a grate, two Poles are sleeping on cardboard that they got from somewhere. Around the station sleep-deprived people are milling about: a black woman, a Russian, a Pole, a Ukrainian, two or three crazy Italian women and a Lithuanian.

In the morning Charlie and Mick went back to Fiumicino Airport. There you can sit in the lounge all evening. There are toilets, and above all—big ashtrays full of butts waiting to be collected. One can go without eating, but not without smoking.

Paul has a better sense of smell, because he has given up smoking. But Mick is smoking again.

One lounge, another lounge, a third lounge.

Jagger and Watts had already been arrested three times. They had fake passports, so after questioning they were released. The Police promised to let them phone someone, but later other policemen didn't let them. Scoundrels. Italians are the lowest scoundrels.

Watts was gathering up bits of food left on the tables in the airport's pizzeria. A marvellous place, the airport. You can get a smoke, you won't die of hunger, people leave bits of uneaten pizza, you can sit down and snooze. But after two weeks of this, Jagger got a twitch. He was coughing. Two weeks without sleep—that's a lot.

Jonas Mekas was filming all the Fiumicino adventures. What a nightmare! Some student from England gave Jagger a razor to shave with in a fountain. He had no soap, it was a painful shave.

Then he got the itch. He was scratching himself for two days, not knowing what was wrong. He tried to have a wash in the airport's washroom. Someone offered him some loose change so he could buy some scabies ointment.

He went back to Rome and took a seat in a train awaiting departure from Termini Station. It was going to Naples, by the sea. It took him two trips to get there, because half way there the ticket-checker booted him off the train.

At a beach Jagger and Watts washed their clothes and rubbed their bodies all over with sand, thus getting relief from the itch after a week of suffering. But now their shoes were rubbing and the ten kilometres a day that they walked were like the suffering of Napoleon's soldiers on their way back from the Russian campaign. It hurt a lot. A bleeding big toe, with dislodged nail. Somewhere they stole some shoes, somewhere else (three times) they stole bikes. And so they travelled, looking for food in rubbish bins.

They travelled 50 kilometres on bicycles. At a few petrol stations they cleaned car windows for a while to earn a *Snicker* bar each for the day.

He called Annette with a phone card. He said it was best to pretend you're demented, and try to live like that, because there are quite a few demented

46

people among the immigrants.

So that's what it's like to travel in the lowest class. It became clear that Mick had got a fungal infection of his toenails. Watts had to carry Mick on his shoulders. They had lost hope in their ability to withstand the immigrant lifestyle.

Three times they had their fingerprints taken, ten times they were arrested and several times they got to sleep in cells that were full of fleas.

Milan railway station is locked up overnight, so they had to shuffle about to keep warm, sometimes getting on a bus to the outer suburbs just for the chance to snooze.

Twice they got something to eat at a welfare centre near the jail, a great place for those who had still not learned to cope with freedom. For two months they rattled around Italy on trains, getting thrown off by the Inspectors about every 50 kilometres. Most often they crawled under the benches of the railway carriage. They kept still, so that no one would hear them. It was also possible to get some sleep there.

In Rome there is a railway station near a cemetery. Mick was sleeping soundly there on an old sofa someone had dumped. That was the station from which buses left for Eastern Europe, Poland, Czechoslovakia. But if you had no money, the drivers had nothing to discuss with you. How brutal you have to be to refuse to help a fellow human being so deeply in difficulties! But there is no help to be had in Italy. Embassies are overrun with emigrants—their nationals— in difficulties and they do not have the money to help in each instance. So who else would ever help them?

Twice Jagger and Watts got a meal at a help centre for ex-prisoners not far from Termini station. And once at Caritas. When you have an English passport you can't expect much more.

Jagger had an idea: sugar has calories, and you can get it in almost any café. They got by for two months eating almost nothing else but mouthfuls of sugar. Eventually barmen started to hide it from them. If it weren't for that sugar, they would have died of hunger.

They crapped in the piazza, in full view of many people. In the tunnels too, where all the bums crapped.

Being a bum—that gets you one star under the rubric "Meals, sleep, clothes, transport, domestic requirements".

The Rolling Stones lived through the experience and made a film about it.

❋ ❋ ❋

(Written by the Spaniard)

—Is it horrible? Keith Richard asks the girl.

—Oh, yes, she replies. That's what it means not to listen to your mum. I feel sorry for Jagger. He is a real hero.

Gallows, campfire, and a Russian-speaking Grim Reaper as wise as a woman convinced that these days it's essential to carry condoms.

❀ ❀ ❀

(2. One of us, not one of us)
(Written by the Pole.)

Re: sleep.

At nightfall the question is: where to sleep? In an old rundown building lives a group of welfare-recipient immigrants. On a wooden bench on the third floor of that building, Jagger has fallen asleep. In the morning the other residents called the Police, fearing for their children. They took Mick's fingerprints, and when he was arrested that evening, some other policemen on a different shift fingerprinted him all over again.

Willy-nilly, emigrants start to talk about suffering, having reached the nadir in their search for happiness. We find peace only there, where we are among our own, and we are wanted. In a foreign country our dignity is inevitably diminished. As emigrants we lose the ability to contemplate our Hotel, our dear ones and our haunts, our own places. Memories—they are the basic unit, the monument that we visit so often, as often as we can.

Imagine your own child in Jagger's or Watts' situation.

Annette, who shared her moral dilemmas with Jagger, came to love his strong character, especially his conscientiousness in solving nightmarish problems.

Yes, he was a hero.

His and Watts' friendship became very strong. What they went through united them with inseverable bonds.

Annette started to fall in love with Jagger without quite realising it. Jagger started to fall in love with Watts without quite realising it.

The just god Perkūnas (he of the rolling stones) shows with a severe gesture how it's not easy to flounder about at the one star level, how hard it is, especially until you get used to being without a cent (in two months in Italy, Jagger only got 20 euros in alms), and without sympathy or understanding.

Jagger's and Watts' survival instinct (Pan mentality) helped them to survive, as if they were forest creatures. Hunger, starvation, pain, and above all, lack of sleep (two weeks without sleep, except for maybe only a few moments in the lounge of Fiumicino Airport), and all that among people who have pockets overflowing with money.

There are two mental dimensions: the logical—for science, traffic rules, etc.; and intuition—which is parapsychological, and strongly present in plants, living creatures and animals.

Watts and Jagger were testing out their animal instincts.

48

Munich Central Station has bread crusts for bums and sugar to be stolen by bold thieves. The Bus Station in Munich has a wooden bench that is great for sleeping. Munich Airport isn't suitable either for getting something to eat or for sleeping; there is a big bridge over the Rhein, you can even drink from the river. There were suburbs they tried to go through and got held up by the Police, but they got a great mattress in the nick, and a warm place to sleep. There was a suburb where Russians lived in a block of flats, but they hated bums. Streets with bourgeois houses, like barracks. A cinema where you could pinch some sugar from the buffet. The Munich Olympic stadium, where one time they were treated to apples, but another time they got a knuckle sandwich for trying to help themselves to the apples. A river with a bicycle path alongside, but muddy water (they didn't drink from that one).

The last tram stop in Vienna, a park, sleeping next to the graves of heroes. A bloody nose from a whack by a policeman, sleeping on a bench in a bus shelter. The Embassy in Vienna. No help. In Graz, a youth dance at an old castle and five euro handout to keep an eye on them as they slept under the stairs. Vienna airport, great trains, no inspectors. In the middle of the old town of Graz, a super nosh-up at a soup kitchen for old bourgeois down on their luck.

A bus trip to a suburb of Graz and 10 euros from a person who had a heart. He brought us back to town and dropped us at a tram stop. Two weeks in a boarding house, with food and a bed.

Little towns of one storey houses near Munich. A dingy forest and pond from which you could drink the water.

Breaking into a Jeep to sleep. Breaking into an Alfa Romeo to sleep. Breaking into some other kind of Italian automobile to sleep.

Sleeping in a rowboat on a canal.

Breaking into some sort of flat and taking showers, since they were starting to notice each other's stench. Three arrests in Rome, five in Augsburg and Munich. A visit to a Munich hospital, where they declined to treat the toenail fungus. Two fights with policemen who went too heavy on Watts and Jagger. Train trips from Venice to Rome, Graz to Vienna, Milan, Naples, etc.

A trip through the Alps on bicycles alongside a nice mountain stream. Another bike trip, this time along a forest path into the mountains.

Three trips and some sleep under a bench in a three-bench railway compartment.

Switzerland. A station by a lake. Police checking documents. Milan Airport, where they were robbed. A Russian woman, who offered to let them sleep in the Milan railway station. A castle in Munich, lots of tourists. In the Alps, by a stream, sleeping on a table tennis table in some sort of boarding house, where there were lots of Russian speakers. Three lord-like days in another boarding house. Sleep, meals.

Getting on a train in Vienna, which was going to Munich.

Sleeping on a rug in a corridor of some library.

49

Being offered kebabs by some students. We waited and waited, but finally got them. That was in a suburb of Munich. In Italy—it's all about money. Very hard to get by without it. The people are bad.

The centre of Munich with two churches.

An abandoned piece of pizza.

A pederast at Termini station, in Rome.

Another pederast in Austria, who called the police when they asked him for bread.

Documents inspected about ten times.

Routes, roads, highways, viaducts, bridges, tunnels, corns on the feet, toenail fungus, limping and suffering.

The militaristic aura of German cities; a construction site shed where they found half a bottle of beer; a construction site shed from which they stole some working boots.

A suburb of Rome, with a social chapter, but they didn't get anything out of it.

Immigrant poetry, which speaks of their essence, of their origins.

❀ ❀ ❀

A refugee camp in Austria, near Innsbruck, five kilometres from the fine alpine resort of Seefeld

(1. meals, clothes, sleep)
(Written by the Pole.)

The Winter Olympics have been held here twice. Alpine forest, outstanding beauty, white peaks on all sides, fantastic sunrises and sunsets, creeks, springs, swans in the courtyard of the boarding house, sheep of various kinds, horses, and about 50 places for migrants awaiting a decision of the Immigration Service on their applications for Austrian citizenship.

There were six Georgians. Some of them worked as masons, others stole. There was an Afghan with his family, an Iraqi with his family, three Turks, ten Africans from Nigeria and some other Africans. There were two blacks from Jamaica, who spent their evenings in Seefeld dancing in a bar. Dancing—that's all they want out of life. There was a young thief from Moldova. All his relatives came to visit him, they slept on the floor. The boss was tolerant. The kitchen was ideal; there was food, showers, forty euros for cigarettes. Just live and enjoy. After their wanderings, Watts and Jagger washed up here.

Every day they walked five kilometres uphill to Seefeld and five kilometres back. McCartney and Bill Gates were there, staying in the hotel's best luxury suite. McCartney had come to fence with Jagger. But he wouldn't give him any money, not even for cigarettes. According to him, Annette forbids any concessions, saying that if you start this immigrant experiment you have to see it through properly, as an immigrant.

On the way to Seefeld there are stables and horse pastures. Also hotels, guest houses, bars, cafés, a thousand year old church, great music played by Czech migrants, Tyrolean singing, everything great after the Italian nightmare.

Nobody recognised them. They continued to live *incognito*.

The Moldovan had not been home for two years. The Russians had started families here.

Half the immigrants were from the former USSR. The other half were from Africa.

Do the Austrians need this? No.

There are a lot of boarding houses like that. The Iraqi was transferred to another boarding house, closer to Innsbruck.

✸ ✸ ✸

(1. Meals, clothes, sleep, domestic requirements)
(6. Work, profession, sport, culture, tourism.)
(Written by the American)

Jonas Mekas' voice behind the picture.
America, America, America.

Three star way of life. I, Jonas Mekas, in America. In one room with an Armenian, a blackass from Yerevan.

Algis! Along with Strielčius, Artovas, Kapralas, Aksomas and Mokasinas—you once made Kaunas notorious... Where are you now? Some in England, some in America. Liešćius is in Spain.

Red-faced, as if you had just won the pie-eating competition, you take the envelope. Algis, for a week of dirty work you got paid more than at home. But for twelve hours, twelve hours a day!

(6. Profession, work, tourism, sport, culture. Sergeant.)

—You like this bit? Mick asked Annette in the smoking room at Haare.

—Yes, it's exactly the one I like, replied Annette, taking pride in her taste and in having the upper hand.

The group was not big, but it was very economical. The Pole was neighing. The Ukrainian karate expert was looking for somebody to cross him, and the chess master took his board and chessmen everywhere he went, making fun of

51

the hippy ideology.   Travel, exotica—all that is for people of limited intelligence. And what is Rock? Hippies are wrong about that too. After this move Mick became thoughtful: maybe the hippie era was indeed the work of idiots?

Profession? Dishwasher. A Mexican, working together with Jagger. The Jimmy Hendrix of dishwashers.

The Coordinator—the Siamese twin Annette, the beautiful author from Germany.

Jagger and Watts are sitting in the back of the Jeep. In the front seat, next to the driver, am I—Jonas Mekas.

Annette phones from Munich to pass on an action verdict. A notice in a Lithuanian newspaper: "Employment opportunity in USA. Caring for invalid boy. Jūratė". Meeting point: L.A. International Airport.

Jūratė is already an American citizen. She doesn't pick up the phone for a long while.   Then she says to call back later, because her live-in boyfriend Kęstas got a black eye from a Puerto Rican in an Indian bar last night, so because of his shiner he doesn't want to go to the supermarket, where he despises the American beer, but what can you do? And so forth.

So Jūratė came for Jagger, Watts and me about three hours later, and she said:

—He'll be a little bit of bother, but not too much, you'll manage, even if you haven't had any real challenges in life yet. Like a mild dose of the clap—not much of a problem.

(Re: 1. Meals, clothes, sleep, domestic requirements. Sergeant)

In this dump, where a lot of Lithuanian immigrants to the USA gathered, they slept seven to a room in a black neighbourhood. The nearest telephone—a kilometre away. Jūratė will find all seven of them a job for a fee of one thousand dollars each: a job washing geriatric bums, or working in a kitchen, or a construction site, whatever.

After the flight from Europe, Jagger didn't know whether it was day or night. He couldn't sleep for three days. For those three days a Jewish-run firm looked for work for him, because the child-minding job for the invalid boy went to an Armenian, who had arrived a day earlier.

—We are still young Jagger told Meda, who was already into the second week of waiting for a job as a nanny. But at the last minute Jagger decided not to have sex with Meda: seven witnesses—maybe too many?

What with paying extra for sleeping at night, and extra for food, the wallet was getting emptier, and still no work in sight. Spend all your money, and how will you get back to Europe?

52

In the office the Jewish girls are busy on the telephones. If they find you a job, you will pay them a percentage. The women from Lithuania don't speak Lithuanian. Or don't speak at all. It's not necessary for women working as housekeepers.

(1. Sleep—like a sergeant, seven to a room)

Disturbed rhythm, no energy to grovel. But better than sleeping in the street.

The Coordinator Annette gives Jagger a chinwag: meals, sleep, domestic requirements—two stars, work—one star.

In Lithuania the parks' ponds and paths are full of yellow leaves. In California, 'nature' is phoney: palm trees planted in imported dirt. In California, 'nature' has the aura of a pretty prostitute. No sincere charm. Pretty, but... — something's missing.

A little job in Santa Monica: cutting the lawn next to the Conservatorium of Music, scratching the weeds out of the pavement. Then four empty days. A swimming pool to be cleaned. Not a lot of money to be earned, but the work is not hard, compared to some other odd jobs.

Finally a message: a 'physical' job was available in Sacramento. Five star hotel with three restaurants. The job is in the kitchen, which is for common use for the whole hotel. This is where the virtuoso Mexican dishwasher works. Jagger invites Coordinator Jonas Mekas to help. He lives in an apartment with some Armenians. They need someone who speaks Russian. Seven of them live in a three-room apartment. They use the swimming pool twice a day. I phone Lithuania and I boast: an apartment with a swimming pool. I invite friends to come from Lithuania. For five hundred I promise to find them a job as a taxi driver, or in a pharmacy or suchlike. New immigrants are exploited by the earlier immigrants. The Jewish people at the office say that's why people came out of their cave dwellings, so that they could fill their heads with new ideas, ideas that lead to a belief in the dollar as the principle of communism. You will be very happy, but stick with it until you win, overcoming all obstacles, until you reach the finish line, the pension, the retirement income or a suitable sum.

You have some money and you down 50 grams of hard stuff just to check whether the bees still fly from your hive into the forest.

The Los Angeles Lakers won the NBA and a huge black man jumps shouting out of a convertible *Ferrari*, and you ask him: son, when you grow up, would you like to be Martin Luther King?

(4. Sergeant: work, profession, tourism, culture, sport)

At 6:30 a.m. a co-worker arrives in a government jeep and takes me to the hotel. At exactly 7 a.m. you enter your number code and stick your fingers down to be read by a scanner. That's how they make sure that you are conscientiously working the whole day. The tempo over the twelve hours is such that you only

53

manage to have three smoke breaks. A bar the length of four tables, loaded with dirty dishes. 'You needn't think you can overwhelm me', you seem to be telling the table. High piles of dirty dishes. You work with special gloves, but the chemicals still affect your hands and make them swell up. There is an automated dishwashing machine, all you have to do is load trays of dishes into it, should be laughably easy. But no: you are all wet, you have splashes all over the checked outfit that the boss provides for all his workers. I, Jonas Mekas, used to change my clothes twice a day. Jagger finds a spot in the courtyard to lie down on some boxes and grab some shut-eye. He can't sleep at night, there's a five-lane highway to Los Angeles right next to his apartment. The din is too loud even for a *hard-rocker*. He can't sleep.

The Mexican is a virtuoso. The former bantam-weight boxer tosses the boxes around irascibly and emphatically. This is his battle arena. The Administrator and the Director gaze respectfully on his noisy and emphatic work. When the mountain of dishes disappears, he washes the doors with a cloth—he is always on the move. In the army you have to always look busy, even when there is no real work. It's hardest when there are special orders, banquets. There's not enough room for the dirty dishes, there's so many of them. You have to hurry, because more and more are on the way. You get a fright. You can be told off for poor work and you can be dismissed on the spot. I saw how they sacked a Filipino in an eyeblink. So then it's back to driving for hours to get to Jūratė's place in L.A., back to living like an animal and waiting for a job opportunity. All that costs money, so again you're afraid: will I have enough money to go home?

The Armenian is talking on the telephone with a Lithuanian who has found his way to Florida. The latter is crying openly and begging the other to send him a few dollars, because he cannot even phone home to arrange for money for an airfare to be forwarded to him so that he can return to Lithuania. He is crying. The Armenian is laughing. Some time ago in Florida he talked away this Lithuanian's telephone card. Now he's laughing. See that? Shall I uncork this baby? The wine is French, he says, with fear in his eyes.

In San Francisco there is a survey of people seeking asylum in the USA. Each paid one thousand to a lawyer. He writes up the papers. They coach you what to say. They hire an interpreter. The five Armenians—every one of them was claiming religious persecution. All of it is a bluff. But the lawyers smile a crooked smile and nod their heads when the Armenian talks with tears about his problems in Armenia. He shows a scar (it's a bluff, sheer bluff). And the tears are a sham. These fellows are former drama students.

There is a Committee in San Francisco, where the nearest political refugee centre is. How happy the Armenian was on returning from there! Yes, a green card. It can be won by anyone who has enough brains and craftiness. America, America. The Armenian has dreams of opening a little restaurant. He brought home from the hotel the recipes of everything they serve. He is selling his flat in Armenia. He aims to become a wealthy American. For the moment he continues to wash dishes, and he tells you—albeit quietly—that he works just as

54

well as the Mexican, who is coming on Sunday with his kids, to show the boss his commitment.

The hotel has a café-restaurant smorgasbord. It has everything from cakes to all sorts of salads and fruits.

(1. Food, clothes. Here Mekas, Jagger and Watts are at a General's level.
4. Profession, work, tourism, culture, sport—Sergeant's level; meals—General's level)
(Written by the American)

The work is so hard, in the heat you lose your appetite. *Coca Cola*, S*prite* and some other drinks are cold, you can drink as much as you want, but you have no appetite. The more you drink, the more you sweat. It's very hot in Sacramento.

Hear that? Yes, yes, you will say, and I go on describing this hell in paradise.

Coca Cola is a good drink. I think it may have been invented by Egyptians, those fellows who sleep in the shade of pyramids. I have stains under my armpits. I am splattered with grease. I change into a new uniform. This time, the pants are not my size, but never mind.

Jagger is showing great sporting form. But this is not the worst hell he has seen. In one minute you make sixty movements, and the trays are heavy. You have to keep moving, keep moving.

One time I tried to read a newspaper in the smorgasbord restaurant. The boss warned me with a waggling finger. Cultivating one's mind is not something that need concern manual labourers.

—Yes sir. I hear you, sir. Thank you very much, sir.

My black workmate snaffled the key from the store room and he goes in there to sleep. When you are in sight, you have to work. If you hide, who knows—maybe you were sent on an errand?

Wash out four refrigerated store-rooms, three other rooms, the tables, cutlery. Scrub that table until it shines! Everything has to be as clean as on a battle-ship. And the work conditions are similar. Over twelve hours you work yourself into exhaustion.

The whole time you're afraid. Fearful of losing your job and ending up in a queue with other bums for bread and a place to sleep. It can happen to anyone. The tension is endless. America, America...

Take note: meals. Clothes, domestic requirements: here I am a General. Work, profession: here I am a Sergeant.

Jagger and Watts sleep in the end room. They can smell the blacks from the first floor. Next to the shower room is the room where Hasmik and Karena from

Yerevan sleep, and Sofi from Iran. They are Armenian women who have left their family at home; they work as chambermaids in the motel. In a few minutes they tidy up the rooms and vacuum the dust, they clean the bath tub and the toilet bowl. Their hands are all calluses. The work is hard, although Hakop, an Armenian who sleeps in the kitchen next to me, claims that he could do that work twice as fast, and that our work is really hard, whereas the women's work is a joke.

Hakop likes to chat before falling asleep. He talks about his 'studies'. He got an economist's degree in Moscow as an 'extra-mural student', by delivering cognac to his lecturers. He didn't really need to study. He bought his assessments and exam results. He told how once in Yerevan they called him to the military commissariat and told him that he will be sent to Georgia, to a paratrooper training base. It was the Brezhnev era and paratroopers were being sent to Afghanistan, where they would descend on houses in Kabul and start machine-gunning everyone in sight, women and children included, and old people, on the grounds that they might be armed.

It was a coup d'état. Yes, he killed some people and now he doesn't feel too good about it.

He told how he was a butcher during the Moscow Olympics. He had lots of cognac supplies. That enabled him to screw half the women in the athletes' residence.

—Have you already been to my place? he would ask the Russian girls that came to knock on this fine Armenian's door. If you've already been here, bye now. But send one of your girlfriends that hasn't been here yet.

He did half the residence. Then he brought over the militiamen from the neighbouring barracks, who were supposed to be providing security for the Olympics... The Russian girls weren't as happy to screw with them as they were with the Armenian, but what the heck, everybody was satisfied.

In his view, they drafted him into the paratroopers to be sent to Afghanistan because of his service in special units in East Germany. He said there was a German who used to come to their unit's logistics warehouse in Berlin, who had not one hair on his bum. He said he couldn't control himself, nor could all the soldiers from the Caucasus, who screwed the German all week because of his hairless bum.

Hakop got a green card and changed his name. He dreamed of getting a pension from Moscow too, and returning to Yerevan and living with his American dollars. His idea—the Refugee Commission—the persecution of Armenians in Nagorno-Karabach and Baku. He got so carried away with his tall story that tears welled in his eyes.

The Iranian–Armenian woman brought me some sport shoes and some shorts from the motel. It's not only vibrators and other sex toys that scatter-brained Americans leave behind. Karena said that modesty forbid her from telling all. Some of the things she had seen...

56

Sofi paid her lawyer a thousand dollars and he was preparing her documents for getting a green card on the basis of religious persecution and other problems. It was all a bluff.

A Lithuanian lass in Lithuania hunted herself an American. When they arrived in the USA, he made her reimburse him for what he had spent on wooing her. He made her live in the garage. She sued and now she has no money to return home. Furthermore, she had sold her flat in Lithuania.

Sofi says that another way to get a green card is through a bogus marriage. But in many cases, once they get the money they don't follow through, they deceive you.

Quite a few immigrants come to the USA via Mexico. Bus drivers bring illegals into the USA for a fee. To cock a snoot at the law is every immigrant's goal. At Brighton Beach, the Russian Jews don't work. Why should they? They can get by on welfare.

Hakop's snoring makes the walls shake. Jagger can't fall asleep in the flat opposite. There is a constant roar from the highway below the window. America—it's a leaky flat that wants to have an image like a tough cowboy (e.g. Charles Bronson). In this place you need optimism like a patient needs a bed. Thank you, sir. I'll look after that myself, sir.

Hakop recounts how one time he fired a gun in the air to frighten off some black housebreakers. They are cowards. You have to use force with them to avoid becoming their victim.

For five dollars Hakop had sex with a mixed race woman he claims was not bad. Business rats with chattering teeth—isn't that what America is called? Two possibilities: let the pig go or fight the rats with a stick. Let's leave this thought for a little later. Life is as hysterical as a lemon.

Breeds? Roses? Have you seen many black chess grandmasters? Their racial feeling sticks to them like chewing gum to a moccasin.

Two twos are four. Through the haze of pretty sentences you will see life's decathlon. Make a plan in the morning. Do that instead of exercise.

I, for example, work to save money for the future. For my good reputation (immigration study). For hedonism (swimming pool, *Coca Cola*, beefsteak, beer). For friendship, love, sympathy. I followed the example of Jagger, an English gentleman from London, and Charlie Watts, also an English gentleman from London. We became friends.

Profession. Imagine that I am very talented and I will manage to make lots of films, turning them out like *cepelinai*—big Lithuanian dumplings.

Being first. I have to make every effort to be better than Mick Jagger and Charlie Watts at washing dishes. Objectively better. It's something to worry about. I will do it. Maybe because of my provincial outlook. For the moment I am the silliest face in the circus toilet's mirror. Mick has already done a few pyramids, I haven't. I believe that future movie audiences will yet do subtle oohs and aahs for me. My belief in myself is sacred, along with my starched white shirts. My belief in myself is noble, like the American flag. In this era of skinny cows and mad cows you cannot afford to have any less faith in yourself.

I am enjoying a surge after the reality of the unspoken swearwords harboured against me.

Sofi the Iranian–Armenian woman is paying a lot of attention to me. She is plump, not young, but who will take an interest in an immigrant? Only another immigrant.

Annette. I think about her every day. What is to be done? How can it be helped, that my fantasy is in a plaster cast? The Russians are to blame. This is what a very hungry and very angry Jonas Mekas tells you, and he is the toughest of the run–fetch boys in America.

Hakop told us how one time in Yerevan he picked up a beauty half his age. He humped her for a long while, with much success. She didn't like him. Finally he achieved victory, determined as he was to be such a powerful lover that the girl had no choice but to capitulate and say "yes, in bed there is none better than him". He is practical, not an idealist.

His ambition is a daily thing, like his white shirt, which he wears daily as a matter of principle ever since the time he worked as the manager of a big shoe emporium in Leninakan. Now in Sacramento he has a Bulgarian woman, who is also forced to admit: "yes, in bed there is none better than him".

Hakop's father was Jewish, his mother Armenian. A good breed. Hakop was the best Armenian I ever met in my life. As proud as a lion, but with the gentle smile of the Mona Lisa, he hooked up with an Italian woman in the hotel kitchen's supply room, and that Italian woman acknowledged that, yes, he was something special. And there in the refrigerator, in the sub-zero temperature, he bent her over and had sex with her. I walked in on them, and later the Italian woman used to save me a piece of chocolate cake, so that I would keep my mouth shut.

Charlie Watts scrapes the frying pans, cleans the ovens with chemicals, all wet with sweat, half lying down, he polishes the stove, while the cook (a Turk, I think) points with his finger and says "rub this bit some more". The kitchen boss brings some Mexican food. The Mexican is revered here. Twelve hours non-stop he works, all action. The Administrator, Bob, on his way past throws me a "So, how's it going?"

He can tell that Charlie Watts, Mick Jagger and I are out of our element. As he looks at me trying with all my might to get on top of the mountain of plates, it's as if he's saying: "Want a dollar? Everything OK?"

"I'll send you to Siberia", says Administrator Bob to me.

The Mexican toils away shining the door of Bob's office.

Here the hierarchy is clear-cut. The Mexican is a slave, and a good one because he doesn't try to be more than a slave.

I learned how to work too. The head waiter noticed it, and the manager noticed it. My goal was to be better than the virtuoso Mexican, whom I also accepted into my mental hotel. He is one of the hundred that were once dwelling in my soul, in my mental hotel.

If you have dealings with a person 30 times, whether you like it or not, you remember him and accept him into your mental hotel. Rattling along with my

58

mental hotel, I travel the 11 routes. I try to get a good reputation at work. The Filipinos with their soft smiles get the cushy job of delivering meals to the guests' rooms. But they gild the lily by telling people they are highly qualified workers. They work in several places, because they have to maintain their families. So they save their energy; to some extent they only pretend to work hard.

Hakop came to blows with a black fellow who was avoiding real work. The blacks were afraid of the Armenian. Hakop used to do wrestling for a sport. But in his heart he has the American dream: his own business, and his own house with a swimming pool.

I caught a tram to the bus station, and from there a taxi (an old beat up car, the door handle came off in my hand) to the Polish lawyer's place. The taxi driver brought me there and led me right to the office door of the Polish lawyer.

My story was to be: anti-Semites are picking on me because I associate with Jews. Friends from Lithuania will send me a doctor's certificate to say I was beaten up and persecuted. I would allege that Jews are not welcome in public places. Whereas Americans are all in favour of freedom and democracy. Migrants from various countries make use of this. On my way back, a French woman showed me where the bus stop was. She was married in the USA, but she did not appear to be very happy.

I was looking for a newspaper with job advertisements. A Japanese woman, a restaurant administrator, showed me where there was a newspaper vending machine. What was she doing here? She seemed tired and unhappy.

The pace of work in the USA is incredible. Even for the Japanese it's too much.

I am a student of the eternal Grand Ambition Academy, so I tolerate America, which has the character of Wagner, without the talent of Mozart. The dollar, that demonic hedgehog of civilisation, grinds you in a flask with spirit and hangs you out to dry and shrivel. The American dream of a family, house, a couple of cars, a good job—it all is hung out to dry and shrivel, because it appears that life is too short: you spend each day working for comfort (Colonel's rank), for family (the guillotine of divorce constantly hangs over you), for your career (leadership—a Lieutenant's rank), for love (General's rank), for friendship. (Even the best friend can let you down in the worst circumstances.) For catharsis (which you perform in a bar or in some sort of sect).

American standards and cowboy independence, pluckiness—that's what has been created here over a couple of centuries. The whole world is learning from the USA. And from Hollywood. And here I am working in their interest as if I had an arrangement with them to idealise the *happy ending* ideology. What can I say?—there's no denying that there are things to be learned from them. The standard—it's not banal, it's tried and true. You can invent a bicycle that peels potatoes, but it's better to choose an old, tested standard. Jagger goes into the little room where the uniforms are kept and exchanges his dirty uniform for a clean one. The Filipino wears his uniform in the apartment too, not just in the hotel. He doesn't want to wear out his clothes. For the Filipino head waiter, a former airport mechanic, pensionable age—life is hard. He has a prostate problem—he never earned a pension. He is suffering all this for his grandson, who will try to be a true American, not one who will ever have to try to shave in a fountain with a blunt razor.

The only time and place to socialise on the job is when standing by the door having a smoke.

—What's your name? the black Somali asks Jagger.

—My name is a meaningless noise. It will evaporate and disappear among the cosmic dust and debris.

Bob is smoking and chatting with the head waiter, who is my age. Californian dialect. I feel some sympathy for Jagger, but he's not sure why.

—This hotel, says Bob, belongs to an Armenian who returned home and bought the big "Armenia" in Yerevan. Immigrants often make a career of exploiting less experienced immigrants. The money is in the envelope, the FBI isn't sticking its nose into it, the owner is getting rich.

—The word 'hotel' is our soul, says Jagger. I'm over 50. Over that time I have gathered a bunch of relatives, neighbours, classmates, co-workers, weirdoes, girlfriends and friends. About a hundred in all. They all have different degrees of interest in the decathlon: from Sergeant to General. I love even those that I was once angry at and with whom I had icy relations. They are part of me, residents of my mental hotel. I carry them around with me as I move about and live in this student hostel that we call the Earth. There's no time. Time is standing still.

On the escalator of life you are travelling along eleven paths and you love this student hostel that we call the Earth. Time is your allocation of years, and it gets a fraction shorter every day. There are eleven garden beds that you have to hoe. Eleven routes to be travelled. You decide yourself whether you are going to be a lieutenant or a sergeant. Life will satisfy your ambitions. You will get what you want. You just have to try. Every person is an angel. Every person is a piece of manure. Avoid or choose the positions, wherever they appear.

This student hostel that we call the Earth has a commonality, a sense of belonging, a smell, and a feeling of peace and satisfaction. Six billion novels, all worth a Nobel Prize, are walking around on the Earth. Smell test. Only IQ, beauty and energy are hereditary. All the rest we get in life as we go along. An exact plan, to err or not to err, this is how we row our boat along the eleven canals.

At the door where they smoke there are two chairs. Bob, although higher in rank, is standing. Jagger is sitting. Charlie Watts comes to have a smoke too.

—An immigrant's life is like walking through a minefield, says Watts. You can't force a person to do something for which he has no inner or outer motivation. The error is in the planning. It's all moving—but where is it going? Eleven routes: that's what there is, set firmly and for centuries. But the impudent human race resists wise discipline. Immigration causes changes in your life that wake you up. A trap for superficial sillies. External glow, romanticism and exotica, and sometimes—true beauty.   But does beauty produce a harvest? Hemingway should be tried posthumously for document falsification.

—My father, says the senior waitress, played soccer for Czechoslovakia at the World Championship in Mexico at the same time Pele was there. Now he lives in Chicago.

—Are you married? Are you in love? I asked.

—Love with a capital *L*, says the Czech head waitress, is nicotine addiction. Love with a small *l* is the cigarette that I just smoked.

—Love is what is left when the romantic infatuation is over, said Bob.

—A spermatozoon has about 30,000 bits of genetic information. The whole human race is a rubber stamped global village. When you see someone, if you have the vision of a Rembrandt, you could accurately see which of the 30,000 possible variations is dominant in him.

—I will be as frank as an open cupboard, says Bob. You assess a person and you guess what the person's own assessment of himself is. That's all.

—A woman's hanging gardens, Jagger tells the Czech woman, tell you that the prize being played for is something more than just going to bed together. Am I right?

—I have a boyfriend, I guess I belong to him, said the Czech waitress.

—The greater the treachery, the sweeter the revenge, said the ever-young Jagger. He could mentally smell the flowers growing under a girl's bedroom window. And impressions—they are just adrenalin.

—A woman is like a hotel, a lot of guests spend some time in there, said Charlie Watts. We men want beauty: we want our 'hotel' to be five star. Such a code of behaviour builds tolerance.

Over cigarettes I got chummy with the room cleaner Bill, a young intellectual. I asked him to try and get me an easier job.

—Do you think I have a good job? he replies.

—It's too hard for me in the kitchen, I tell him. He tells me about California's history, about how the Mexican Indians lived here before. He is also interested in John Kennedy's history.

For a young person the future is enchanting and full of unfathomable possibilities. That is the energy that gets us through the rest of our lives.

Charlie Watts and the Administrator, Bob, are chatting about the concept of "One of us–not one of us", which is one of the eleven garden plots or routes of life.

—Our places, our people, our habits—the residents of the hotel that is always with you. Memories are monuments that are close by, at your fingertips. That is the advantage that an immigrant loses. A foreign country will always be foreign to you. The quality of happiness drops off. The exotic allure of emigration pushes people into making mistakes, because the true happiness of knowledge—that means theoretical work at five o'clock in the morning by the light of a lamp. You don't have to become a victim of mosquitoes on the savannah; you can get the pleasure of all the eleven points over the television. Theoretical work saves time and helps avoid mistakes. Information doesn't

61

come only from friends. The press, television, cinema, literature, and people who work in these fields—the information from these sources will help you find the correct solutions.

My aim is to make friends with Charlie Watts. We both idolise Buddy Rich, Tony Williams, Vladimir Tarasov.

Jagger and Watts were living in my apartment block, which consisted of perhaps ten apartments, some of four rooms, some only one room—all ranged around a swimming pool. I phoned Annette and told her that we wanted to finish work tomorrow. In order to decide, we have to discuss it.

We were sitting on a mat by the swimming pool. Jagger was swimming. Annette, on her second day in the USA, was smiling her inimitable smile, as if to say "How sweet you are, babe". She was sitting in her battery-powered invalid scooter, because she did not want to advertise the fact that she was a Siamese twin. Her legs were hidden under a fluffy skirt.

Watts is tanning himself by the edge of the pool. Not far away a black man was sitting in the shade reading a newspaper.

Annoyed by the man's excessive jewellery, Jagger said in a loud voice for all to hear, especially the black man:

—Why are you looking at our woman? I am just trying to defend my colleague. Your gaze is lewd.

— I'm trying, said the black man. What I don't do, God will.

— Are you a gigolo or Alphonse? asked Charlie Watts. Maybe you're impotent, and you waste your money at the sex shop"?

—Young fellow, said Jagger, do you want to eat dung and be kept away from the light for a few years?

—In my glance is the peace of an insect collector, said the black man, as he disappeared.

Our project in America was waving, like a branch of maple being shaken by the wind. We demonstrated cold and objective interest, like the referee in the boxing ring, and it seems that we investigated emigration thoroughly. We had seen the sun coming up black. We had had enough.

Jagger came up to Annette and kissed her neck.

—We just wanted to test our heroism, he said. Now we have to concentrate, because the wind has still not dispersed the *prana* (Sanskrit — the life-sustaining force within the universe) that we got on our project "Those immigrant pigs". But there won't be many wishing to follow in our footsteps...

—I have seen Brian Jones in an SS uniform, said Annette. That insolent Hitler's drive is all too apparent. In their youth the Rolling Stones, by the way, were like they are now: capable fellows, for whom nothing was taboo.

—The smell test says: sharp, clear, subtly fluctuating smell, says Jagger.

Annette smiled as one would to a child that is cute without even trying.

***

62

Jagger.

(Written by the Jew)

Nevertheless, the biggest humiliation I ever experienced was by the Munich Olympic Stadium. An old fellow was selling apples. I was fainting from hunger. Unable to bear it any more, I grabbed an apple and bit into it. The merchant, muttering something in German, punched me in the face, just under my eye. I was very unhappy, convinced that people are selfish and mean.

An inspired person, one who senses smells subtly, melts into the harmony of nature. In this, and in other aspects, he reaches an intuitive solution.

Paul McCartney, his heart raging with love, went to visit Annette in Haare, a suburb of Munich. The Director of Division IX was reluctant to give Annette leave, fearing investigations and Interpol involvement in the work of the drug and alcohol rehabilitation section of the Haare Psychiatric Hospital. She had two months of her sentence left to serve.

Annette attended occupational therapy, where patients assembled various plastic gadgets. The occupational therapist was teasing two Russians, one of whom was of German ancestry and came from Siberia. His surname was Andropov {same as the Premier of the USSR at the time}, which was a cause of great mirth to the inmates. The other Russian was from Saint Petersburg {still *Leningrad* at the time}, and he had a Jewish wife. The Russians were despised by the Germans. The Turks, Serbs and Croats didn't like them either. The southern Slavs sang their ethnic songs, as if to show that they are not inferior— or maybe even superior—to the others. Annette also attended body-building exercises, every second day, and daily ball sports that did not require excessive physical exertion. Twice a week she participated in an Art and Culture group. At Haare there was a great tennis court, but Annette didn't try her hand at that.

The food was good, maybe even five star level. Annette was living in a two-bed ward with a drug addict named Eliza, who read the magazine *Bild* every day in the smoking room. That's where the patients assembled to chat and listen to music, including the Rolling Stones. Munich had 3–4 radio stations, but the music they broadcast was pretty much the same. That day, for example, Annette was listening to *Steppenwolf*, a good old group from the hippie era.

Annette spent most of her time in a construction shed by the main entrance. There she talked to rockers and National Socialist Party activists. That morning when Paul McCartney visited at 11 am he found her at the hairdressers. Going to the hairdresser in Haare is an expensive pleasure, but it is essential for a woman who wants to be beautiful.

Admirers of Annette were always to be found among the thirty or so people being treated in the section, because Annette had a very interesting manner: she mooched cigarettes, she chatted you up, she tried to win your confidence, but over time it became clear that it was just her manner, that she wasn't really a sleep-around, which still didn't prevent her from being admired by almost all the men.

In the shed the hairdresser was extremely happy to have such a generous client and even happier to see Paul McCartney live.

—I love every cell in your body, said Paul.

Feigning a Jewish accent, Annette garbled: —*Stronk* words, *darlink*. Do you like *mein* clothes? We *Juden* respect those who respect us.

McCartney understood the humour and sang a couple of bars of *Hey Jude/ Jew(d)*.

—I must *emphassaiss* that *Auschwitz* is the Germans' idea of *bleck* humour, continued Annette.

—Your manner of speech is Mozartian, said Paul. Because your character is partly melancholic, partly choleric, and it's the best suited for art. And maybe for love too. There are always people around you, they want to see you, to hear your voice. You remind me of John Lennon.

—Well, you remind me of the most beautiful man in the world. There were two candidates—Alain Delon and Paul McCartney.

—Jacqueline Kennedy chose Onassis for some reason, and you're not a beggar either, but you chose me.

—No, says Annette, I chose Mick Jagger, because his character is predominantly choleric. All the brides in the world look to Mick. His reputation at love is... sensational.

—I'm enchanted by your smell, says Paul. I look upon you as if you were the first woman in my life, my first orgasm and my first wet dream.

The phone rings, Annette waits for the hairdresser to leave the room. The telephone keeps ringing.

—Oh, hi Sean, says Annette. Paul is here with me. How are you keeping?

—Tell him regards from Uncle Paul, said McCartney.

—Sean has got in touch with Cat Stevens, says Annette. As you know, he has converted to Islam. That should be useful for us, because Prince Charles wants us to look into the Arabic question.

The joy of his relationship with a Siamese twin propelled McCartney like the wind in the sails of the royal yacht.

—I wink my right eye to you, says Paul. I am the winking absolute.

—Well you remind me of a knight who has lost in battle. What are you, a *man of your word* or a *man of many words*?

—I will zip up my Irish smile with a plastic zipper and my pure clean *'Girls'* sadness I will send to you during the next show that my fans demand.

—*Okay*, said Annette. I'm really wondering, what's better for me, Sean Lennon, or will Paul McCartney really be better.

***

Did anyone recognise Mick? Yes, they did. In the main railway station of Rome there are about four cafés, and when their barmen saw Mick coming, they would hide the sugar. They knew him. And these Italian dorks did not like his survival method of grabbing a few calories.

The U.N.

There is village talk, regional dialect, slang, and then there is literary language. Similarly, people who consider that they are upholding the humanist principle of peer group tend to stick to the literary language, whereas suburban slang—that's the Sephardic or Ashkenazic idea of peer group.

Sean Lennon—a cherry tree in blossom, but master of Japanese martial arts.

Bill Gates mounted the speaker's dais at the United Nations Organisation headquarters with Mick Jagger and Charlie Watts. All three of them. Charlie's eagerness to make an impression was touching (he reminded the public about the principles of 'Ringo Starr's Mental Technique').

—Has emigration decreased in the world? asked Mick. He felt at home on the stage.

—Yes, replied the Secretary–General. Based on our data, the rockers' efforts have been productive. Jonas Mekas' film about the problems of emigrants has received wide coverage on television; a clear victory. Hundreds of thousands of naïve romantics and seekers of materialistic advantage have been saved from themselves.

—I am a fighter, says Gates. In everything I do I am ready for battle, victory or death. Non-stop pressure in each of the 11 points of life values. I come out into the *dojo* psychologically prepared to do or die. What's more, I feel pleasure in the battle. Folk customs and standards require particular skill to separate the banal from the worthy. My choice for physical culture: the rapier. Maybe that's why I find it easy to prepare for battle. Maybe that's why I find something to talk about with the half-Japanese Sean Lennon. John washed his nappies, but we accept him into the company of us rough men. Never before have I felt to be on such a good team—Annette Hess, Charlie Watts, Paul McCartney and Jonas Mekas. Negotiations are very productive when they are among equals, all with above-average IQs. For example, Sean began to cry when his German Shepherd dog, who he called 'B.B. King', died. And I'm not giving that fact undue prominence. The dog had coordination, energy, and beauty, plus it was dedicated to its master. We are also dedicated: dedicated to rock and roll and the blues, dedicated to all the eleven points of 'Ringo Starr's Mental Technique', especially the one "friendship, love, sympathy", and

65

dedicated to the whole student hostel that we call Earth. We call upon the leaders of the G-8 nations to support the "Empire of the Arts" idea. You have seen how our work is producing results. Hundreds of capable and talented people are behind us. Our fuehrer Annette Hess supports the ideas of capable and talented cinematographers, literati, musicians. We want something concrete—a city-state with several quarters, and for that we need some cooperation, which is where the intercession of the U.N. would be helpful. Druskininkai, Yalta and Svetlogorsk are three candidates. A farmer manures the land, works it, cultivates it, reaps a harvest, and finally—we eat bread. In our venture likewise we need to work out possible combinations of moves.

Private interest—bigger result. It should be that politicians do not have any private interest. Philanthropists and artists mostly have a vocation; a fanatical love for their profession. But in practice that doesn't happen much. Let's vote. Who is in favour of the creation of an 'Empire of Art'?

Only the Georgian and Lithuanian parliamentarians raised their hands.

—Ladies and gentlemen, said Sean Lennon, Yusuf Islam, previously known as Cat Stevens, became a Muslim in 1978. He has told me about Córdoba, a city in Spain where the huge cathedral is actually a converted mosque. For more than four hundred years people have prayed in there together; there is no conflict of religious mentalities. We should learn from the Arabs. When we look at the Catholic, when we look at the Arab, we should remember their mothers' hearts. We have all had a mother who suckled us and loved us. Can those mothers be friends? My mother is Japanese. Does that mean I should not get on with my brother Julian, who is a Christian?

Members of the Arab culture in the Middle Ages would have had the right to treat Europeans like barbarians. They were more advanced at everything. But did they humiliate or try to convert the Catholics? No. They were tolerant. We should also love the Iraqis, Iranians and other Muslims. They will feel our love straight away and changes in world events will follow. Who antagonises Muslims against Jews? Some fanatical Jews fight against Islam, but they condemn German Nazis while behaving in much the same way as them. Extremists flourish in those spaces where there is no love. Extremist vibes are transmitted to others. The refugee question is of concern to many organisations, but they do not draw a line between Islam and Catholicism, which was the fundamental idea in world politics in recent times. Catholicism and Islam can be united on the basis of the Abrahamic principles of faith. Catholics and Muslims are—or should be—partners. The question of Jerusalem, and Israel's right to exist, are thorny questions for Islam. If a new Shakespeare were to appear and create a film or book to solve this in an attractive way, it would save billions being spent on armies and weapons. We have lost interest in the truth. People are trying to 'reform' religion by demolishing their foundations: married priests, homosexual marriage and so forth. It's the globalists who are organising people to unite in a struggle against Islam. This is extremism not so much in action as in ideas. This is where artists can help a lot. Allocate 200 billion for art and we will restore order. The Qur'an states that Islam must not be forced on people.

66

Christians and Jews, everybody in the world wants to destroy Islam. That is a big mistake. The tripartite Western policy has to be taken off the world stage; the 'Top 50' globalists, who just look after their own interests and benefits, need to be shackled. In the battle for decency the contestants are changing, but its goal remains the same: to do the footwork, to manoeuvre, because decency is— the monotheistic faiths, Abrahamic Islam and Judaism—the Abrahamic religions, the tradition of Isaac, and his son Israel. These religions must unite, and artists have a lot of work to do in these fields. The best protagonists would be a beautiful woman and a very talented artist. The globalists' capital is at work. They participate in management, even when the managers are on holiday or in a circle of bohemians. Capitalism is free competition, that is the ideology of freedom, but globalists want to grab power, which they would probably call revolution. That is a word, but the reality behind it is much deeper and broader. Struggle is what we need, my struggle for ideology, for getting rid of oligarchs, for forming a world view combining Islam and Catholicism. We have to win! We have to convince the globalists that it is not in their interest to be in conflict with Judaism, Catholicism and Islam. And these should unite. Only artists dare to speak this truth. Catholicism unites nations, but intellectuals only unite a small group of people. Different scales. That is why artists have to propagate monotheistic and other religions. For the moment the perspective is not promising. We could end up with genocides like the world has never seen. Whole groups are bought off and it's not feasible to get out of them. The middle class is being destroyed. Only millionaires and paupers will be left. If Jesus Christ was an ordinary prophet, then all religions are equal and good. Live like all the rest. But Catholics have their line. The result of their tolerance is intellectual impotence. Religions have to support the government and the laws. The Pope has an opportunity to unite with Islam. The globalists will hit back with new 9–11s. American secret services working hand-in-hand with Russian secret services. There are just two enemies of globalism: Islam and Catholicism. And it's all done openly, without any secret plot. It's disguised as interests and the masses are fooled. Annette Hess was writing a novel about Islam and Catholicism joining together in a struggle against the globalists, who are acting through manipulation of product costs via middlemen. When people turn away from them, the globalists will lose. Artificial famines are manufactured, as is the market for products, whole continents go hungry. So what's most important is the mind: whether it is enslaved or whether it is free.

Islam and Catholicism will be united by the ideology of tolerance, and by patience. The truth drowns in an ocean of lies. It's hard for a person to get his bearings. The globalists are trying to pit Muslims against Jews and Christians. Judaism is not united and it does not have a hierarchy. Rabbis are not clergymen. They are teachers. Judaism has no organisational backbone. The ideology of Islam is very strong. We have to reckon on that. Judaism is legless and faceless and it automatically follows the globalists, whose interest is in the free market, who keep people below the poverty level.

A feudal society structure is on the way back. As soon as there is a reserve of cheap labour, emigration starts up. And by using cheap labour they put the whole world in thrall. The world's population is controlled through wars, because there shouldn't be an oversupply of serfs. The population is kept in fear through terrorist antic; the entire secret spy force of the USA is bought off. The human race is in a cul-de-sac. The mass media are used to stupefy people. There is an ocean of lies. The whole world is becoming enslaved. Only the morality of religion, particularly the Catholic religion, has a chance to fix the mess. Globalism is a billionaires' ideology. Paul McCartney, Mick Jagger, Annette and myself, we are all millionaires, we are not calculating, we are on the side of the poor people of our countries, as John Lennon said—*Working Class Hero*. History has ended. One language is enough; so is one religion. No countries or ethnicities are required. History has ended. *Viva* globalism!

Memories... Not all people are selfish. One Austrian gave Mick a lift and 10 euros. Maybe about four policemen on separate occasions drove Mick 10, 20 or 30 kilometres.

***

The Lithuanian Jurga Ivanauskaitė leaves the *Euro-2000* Literary Express train to go for a walk around Prague. She was ruminating on the idea of how to get into the billionaires' bank. The goal: the top 50, headed by Gates.

A crowd of people gathered around the cuckoo clock. Tourists from all around the world flock to Prague—one of the most beautiful cities in Europe. You could hardly hear Czech in the street. People were talking Czech in their offices, but outside in the street you could hear Lithuanian, English, Finnish and other languages.

By a beautiful Mozart-era building a kitten was mewing. It was so small that it couldn't even eat yet. Jurga took it in her hands and started to pat it. The kitten settled down.

After half an hour Jurga came back to her carriage and gave the kitten some milk. She had decided. She would bring the creature home, to Vilnius. Maybe it would be her talisman. She had already thought of a name for him: *Praha*.

—Women, said the Russian novelist. They were smoking in the smoking car. The weakest creature is the snake. It doesn't even have any legs. But its poison makes it boss. It's the same with women.

—Let's think about what we're going to write about next, suggested the Georgian litterateur. Maybe about how I screwed socialism and capitalism. That's it: fighting against quack grass—the way of the humanitarians.

—It's raining, said Jurga. A pile of thoughts is falling from heaven— vitamins.

—You are the most capable here, said the Jew. Your father was Jewish. Throw us an idea; we'll vote that you should write the next chapter.

So Jurga threw them an idea, one which she had been carrying around for six months.

—Maybe there are some better writers, but Jurga is the most beautiful among them all, said the German. Everyone in our carriage thought she was beautiful and tried to get close to her. An interesting breed. Her grandfather was Lithuania's foremost literary critic of the Soviet era. He was smart enough to rise to the top, even if he understood that the system was unjust. But it got him a flat, a summer house, a car, prestige. He got everything he could out of the situation—except a good name.

—This moment, said Jurga, I will try to raise my breeding as high as possible. I don't think that in the 21st century there will be a better idea for art. Romanticism—that's false information for superficial youth. Green rue, I beget Alexander of Macedon, so akin to Bill Gates. It is transcendent good fortune to give birth to an idea that will stand the test of time. The highly thoughtful Ringo Starr will bear witness that his Primary School is the highest qualification for a person searching for perfection and the meaning of life. I like to be liked. But for true love you need the sincerity of my kitten, Praha. A person toils for his own sake, for his family, for the nation, for mankind. My idea is higher than Newton, Einstein. It's like telling a German shepherd dog "Go foot it!", a command to the participants at the moment to find something remarkable. For example, ten of Europe's best writers are in love with me. Is that remarkable? Perkūnas struck me and the Rolling Stones began to roll. This idea is a coincidence, and the result of much searching. But Perkūnas did strike me. They say 95% of people believe in a higher power. Science could not find the meaning of life, but art and religion find it. I will give it to Gates if he attacks me.

—Our women! says the Russian. We know how long Mozart's wife was in mourning. She didn't even arrange his funeral.

—We are philanthropists, says the German. We work not for money but for honour. We work by doing battle with the quack grass. It's all registered with God. Perkūnas is severe, but just. A picture by an unknown artist. But it's in the gallery. We have been born for the purpose of writing at least one useful sentence for a writer that is destined to rise to fame.

—I try, said Jurga, to write a sentence after which every one will be dumbfounded, as if they had seen a ballerina with a wooden leg.

The German picks up the kitten Praha and says:

—I will peel off your hide in thin strips, OK? An initiation for SS officers was that they had to cut out a kitten's eyes with a cutthroat razor. I'm almost like them.

—Look, said the Georgian. He was a little tiddly. That chestnut by the house is a little sad.

The *Euro-2000* Literary Express train was crossing Czech territory.

—I'll get a crappy euro out of my pocket and buy a bottle of Georgian wine, said the Russian. I have never had anything against Georgian wine.

—My idea is not short, said Jurga Ivanauskaitė. You lead with the right foot, then the left, and you follow the arc of my idea.

69

—Nonetheless I find you quite beautiful, said the Russian in a wolf-grandmother's tone.

—Let me know when you get tired of my beauty, said Jurga.

—Russians like it, said the German, when a woman is working in the garden and she coos like a dove at the sight of her half-drunk husband.

—From the eleven lines of attack, said the Englishman, you chose the one you want to put your energy into.

Ringo Starr's Mental Technique. Maybe I am quite happy being just a foot soldier in this field and I really don't need to make any effort to rise to General. Complete freedom. Do what you think is best. In regard to the item 'Being first', I, for one, do not participate in it. You can get there before me, but that doesn't concern me. Maybe it would be too easy for me to participate on this front.

The Impressionists' idealisation of the grubby life of the masses, from a certain angle, that's quite remarkable. A special angle for looking at things allows us to idealise a place, a person, history, a certain resident of this student hostel called the Earth. There has been idealisation and hedonistic satisfaction-finding at all time, in all places, with all objects. Of course, to do so requires effort and training. The reward—pleasure in every fragment of life, and a chance to say: "Wonderful!" And to do that every day, every minute. You idealise things around you—trees, flowers, rivers, forests, people—to various degrees in various categories. The mind strives to find wonder, and you manage to be happy, because that which is wondrous is spiritual pleasure. That is hedonism in every case.

This idea saves heaps of money and cuts out lots of hassles.

You can be happy all the time, everywhere, if you just find the right angle from which to view the scene.

Autosuggestion: wonderful. All the people on Earth—wonderful. The Impressionist school—wonderful. The pauper and the General—both wonderful. Life is so variegated, therefore its scenes and participants are... wonderful. All you have to do is try hard, make a determined effort, and you will find something to idealise. Success is guaranteed. You will be saying the word 'wonderful' in even the most banal and impoverished situation. Wonderful. Oh yes! I feel pleasure. Wonderful. It's sunny, it's raining, it's snowing—wonderful!

A country bumpkin—wonderful. An intellectual, a rich person—wonderful. You just need autosuggestion and a certain amount of mental effort. You need to get to understand the Impressionists, who idealised a chair, a sunflower, a little house with an asbestos roof, a prostitute, a beautiful *petite bourgeoise*, etc., etc. Wonderful! Oh yes! I feel good vibes. Wonderful! I am eating the hotel we call Earth and I say—"Wonderful!" Every resident of that hotel/hostel is wonderful. Just adjust the brain and somehow—be happy. The word 'wonderful' is a vitamin, it's a shot of vodka, it's a blessing, in the end —it is happiness itself. 'Wonderful!' It's a *passe-partout*, a skeleton key for happiness. Every day, every resident of 'Hotel Earth' is... wonderful. It's the recipe for happiness: no money required, no real estate, no brainpower, no talent. With the 'Wonderful!' autosuggestion, everyone will find the path, with just a little thought, to feelings of brimful of happiness. It's Einstein. The answer to thousands of mental computations, spat out as if from a computer—get me, this is wonderful. A new effective narcotic and alcohol—'Wonderful!' Note well. Be a student of Cézanne.

A sea of pleasure, just swim through it, and looking around, say 'Wonderful!'

Revolution No. 9. The meaning of life in terms of Ringo Starr's Mental Technique is: calmly battle on those 11 fronts, choosing which you wish to concentrate on and what you want to be, a Sergeant or a General. And the stimulus, the drive, for every five-minute segment of life, is to seek that which is wonderful! This is the philosophical revolution started by the impressionists and the expressionists, and we are all artists, even if not trained in painting, so we notice everything that is wonderful, and we do that which is wonderful.

The meaning of life is the ability to see that which is wonderful. The proletariat and their way of life, the peasants and their way of life, the bourgeoisie and their way of life, the upper class...; everywhere there is something wonderful.

Dizzy from all that wonder, you say: "Yes, I'm happy."

The world is pretty plain, it's like the palm of your hand. With Catholic calm you make plans and quietly implement them. The reward is always right there—wonderful scenes from life on Earth, such wonder!

—I would like, said the Russian, to inoculate such a beautiful and sensible woman at once. So far I have never had the opportunity. But how much does a fly's fart pollute the air?

—Mister, said the Georgian, you're as much use as an empty swimming pool. Let Jurga write the next chapter.

—Hemingway, that romantic shit mincer, said the German, could only dream about a 'Literary Express' like this one. Although he did say: "Artists of all countries—unite!"

—In the time of 'Antanas the Bloody', said Jurga Ivanauskaitė, and in the time of Landsbergis, and the beret women, Lithuanians knew my grandfather, Kostas Korsakas. Since I have become involved in literature, that office of God's symbols, envious people have been throwing my ancestry in my face. Go find yourselves a professor of mathematics who can offer you a better idea.

***

Gallows, campfire, Russian-speaking Grim Reaper.

(Written by J. Ivanauskaitė)

The dead do not dream. Nor do they sleep. I would like to use this campfire for distilling moonshine. It's like sulphur vapours, volcanic smoke, phosphorescent sparks.

Keith Richards says:

—Now I will really scare you, girly. I will introduce you to the manager of the superlaboratory. He is clear-faced, patient, very capable and stubborn.

71

—No need to try and undo our natural inclinations, interjected the Russian-speaking Grim Reaper. Rabble-rousers' inanities. The smaller part cannot recognise itself, or the larger part. That's part of the larger plan. A whole cannot recognise a part that is larger than itself. That's what I have to say about the laboratory manager. And now look at the kitten, Praha. I will prise out his right eye with my knife, so that he will always be one-eyed.

—Dear sir, said the girl, I may not be able to bear such savagery. Listen to me or I'll pour petrol on you and set you on fire.

—OK, said Keith Richards. I'll be refined in my savagery.

***

Mick was in the mountains, sitting on his bike at a traffic stop. Some Russian cyclists pulled up alongside and asked for directions. They were unslept, unshaved and unwashed. He was not the only one suffering from the problems of migration.

***

Jonas Mekas' archival material from the Munich laboratory run by the Georgian Zurab Mšvidobadze

For me, an old Woodstock era rocker, the gold treasure inside the black box of humanity is a concern.

The laboratory is looking for a new form of speech. If art is born from what we see, and ideas from what we talk about, then it's obvious that contours and colours occupy a higher place than ideas, which just follow the scenes from the student hostel of life.

The colour abstractions of outer space, when you close your eyes, run endlessly without repetition. That is one of the principles of the future language. Maybe logic is a *cul-de-sac*? The system of logical reasoning needs to be extended. Feelings, intuition—we learn from our subconscious. Let us use physics formulas and metaphors.

I saw how Zurab Mšvidobadze examined the information in genetic fields in brain cells in his hospital laboratory in the Munich suburb of Haare: with "laser tweezers", not injuring the cellular tissue, examining the microscopic chromosomes and their fragments. Traits to be inherited can be eliminated; for example, the genetic source of a future health problem is identified—and neutralised. When we meditate, we see a changing panorama of cosmos-colours, but they are produced by our eyes, the retinas of our shut eyes. You see forms and colours swimming; it keeps changing, without repeating. If we could come to comprehend such complexity, the possibilities of science and logic would be widened. The time has come to look for new form of speech. Something new. For that, we will need thousands of laboratories, of which maybe only one will find the right path.

You wait, eyes shut, abstractions of colours and volumes, outlines, sculptural elements. Nothing ever repeating itself.

We started in a void. Now we have Ringo Starr's Mental Technique sects operating all over the world. Bill Gates said: "We are priests without cassocks."

Life's legacy is to give birth, urinate, defecate and to make progress in the science and social spheres.

Maybe what's needed to cure chronic diseases is a new science of language.

A gracefully naïve *pas-de-deux*, a sympathetic smile, a dance allegory for a worthwhile purpose—these are the components of Zurab Mšvidobadze's mentality.

Is it true that women are cleaner because they cleanse their blood once a month through menstruation?

The ardour of a shark, king of the fish—that's how Mšvidobadze throws himself into his work. Like d'Artagnan, who in the midst of a swordfight still recited impromptu pieces of his poetry *à la* "Divine Comedy" that he was composing in his head.

Who will make a clay model of a heart-warming birdie? Z. Mšvidobadze. The customary Georgian drive.

But that's just first gear of this racing car.

Just politely have a look at his IQ. He supported the rockers' battle against emigration. Hundreds of thousands of people who have messed up their pension entitlements, who have ended up in the street, millions who have died because of terrible, thankless and filthy work; their kids filling up the psychiatric wards, and the narcotics and alcohol rehabilitation centres... That is the dowry of emigration. You go out into the street and what do you see? A Nigerian, an Arab, a Turk, an Italian, and mostly—Jews.

—Immigrants are uninvited guests, says Zurab (who is also an immigrant, but an invited guest).

—And as the Lithuanian proverb says, guests are like fish; on the third day they start to stink. They are like pirates, and they pass that drive on to their children. They are their countries' partisans, who have parachuted behind the enemies' defence lines. Zurab is more perceptive than the rest, because he lived in both the socialist era and now the capitalist one. Zurab, like Gates, has the charisma of someone with Napoleonic ambition. He makes an effort on behalf of the weak and the poor. The meek, the hungry, the oppressed—his mission is to willingly help cure body and soul.

Purity—that is the Georgian's intention. Peace and plenty in our time, says he. The Russians..., hell, what can you expect from the Russians? The naughty human race resists wise discipline. That thug Hitler was rather unjust. Zurab Mšvidobadze—he is a hard man, part mustang and part tame horse that has submitted to logic and allowed himself to be ridden. Rather like Mick Jagger.

73

"Today I ate only one apple core, which I found in a rubbish bin, even though I walked 15 kilometres. No map, no knowledge of the language, just bleeding feet with a fungal infection of the *nailsss* [said with pain] and a tic from months of lack of sleep. I have the itch, and a fungal infection, I haven't slept horizontally for five months, and the last time I ate a bread roll was five days ago. Today I stole one grape.

Moo moo, I have to shoot you. Moo moo—that's an emigration nickname for old rockers. Migrants are sex maniacs, moo moo—they should be shot.

Zurab Mšvidobadze entered the circle of Mick Jagger and Annette's friends. Like-thinking people, dedicated to Welfare and Humanity.

At the moment, Zurab Mšvidobadze is investigating the subconscious of psychiatric patients and of healthy people in Haare, near Munich. Bill Gates poured five million dollars into his laboratory. This person is—wonderful. The delight of a true hallmark.

Jonas Mekas' material for a documentary film about Arabs

Which face to cry with in the theatre of life? It's the anniversary of John Lennon's death. I still have a lock of his hair. A memento of a sad soul, shoved into a matchbox.

Which one of us would not want a genial, strong, loving father? That's how John was when he rocked Sean. Laws and the Constitution—these are our parents.

To be around Sean Lennon is a bliss. Wonderful, wonderful.

Whatever is grubby—it can be politely left out and not named. John's fooling around—we forgive him it. The old rockers are taking up an unselfish project: they are going to weed out quack grass wherever they see some growing. They wash their money for the sake of their good reputation.

—And what's left?, you will ask. There are many possibilities, but the one you chose is one of the best. It is the age of education—the 21st century. If Joe Lewis lost using an uppercut, that doesn't mean the uppercut is a bad means of combat. That's what education is all about in the 21st century.

Sean Lennon has collected all the material imaginable for an English-speaker about the Arab culture and customs.

When Charlie Watts and Paul McCartney were on a trip to Mecca, Saudi Arabia, they smelled the odour of burning bristles, as if a pig were being singed.

Rod Stewart and David Bowie noticed the same thing. They understood the Arabic soul—a cul-de-sac, they suffer, and they don't get any support, just foreign culture foisted on them.

Peter Handke, a friend of Annette Hess, said he knew a German who had only ever read one novel, and that was in his early childhood. But he was a perfectly affable and charming person. Food for thought. It would appear that literature isn't as important in people's lives as we might think. TV is enough for some.

—Who will we unite in friendship against? asks Sean Lennon. And all of us old rockers feel the tragic quivering of the student hostel we call Earth, where the term *one of us* falls out of the Good Reputation garden bed and gets overgrown with quack grass, like the Arabic incident.

How would it have been, if in his time John Lennon had planted an oak in Paris? Tourists would be crowding around to touch its bark. Same thing with Sean. Everybody loves him, everybody respects him, because John Lennon washed his bum when he was a baby.

To put it in plain language for simple people: Jonas Mekas is coming to Mecca (Makkah).

Soft nipples, longing eyes, nice legs—that is as much Arabian as American. There is no war about that. The war is about petroleum, or to put it differently, about badly invested money.

The Jews, who have a special ethnic smell, are getting in the way of those who are concerned about petroleum.

The song is unhappiness. An Arab in the suburb of a big city asks what his number is. Ninety-eight, a fellow countryman answers him. A week later he asks again what his number is;

—Tell me, because I want to get launched on that most honourable of paths for Arabs. Twenty-two, replies the person who is administering his application to become a suicide bomber.

A precise feeling. Madonna with child. The suicide bomber was once like that, with his mum. Even though we see that we will still want petroleum from the Arabs, while near them sit the former Madonnas with Child. Are not the morality and the code of honour of the student residence at stake? How can we sleep soundly at night, knowing that every day about 20 *jihaddis* die, causing other people's deaths? Let's pretend that we don't see it, that we don't understand it.

The Mozart curve: a principled Arab, an unselfish battle participant from the Mosques where he leaves his *prana*, his aura. People living as they have for many centuries and wanting to do things their way.

It's a sad song.

He died. He died from a tumour. People mostly die from tumours. But not in our time. Now, in our time, they kill themselves, in order to kill others. That's how the words "one of our own" are understood here.

Let's restore order. Let the devil himself do it. He's the one who will have to stand in judgement at God's court, not you. What's important is that he be a good manager.

You may say: Honey is not for the donkey's mouth. Well, maybe. Let him live like a donkey. Freedom to choose. Most blood that has been spilled has been spilled fighting for freedom.

75

Life is like that. You can't take what you want: you have to make do with what you're given. That's a woman's instinct. But aren't women the wisest— and the ones who continue the race? The military leaders of our time display this female-type initiative, all thinking that they are cleverer than each other.

At Haare there was an alcohol dependency patient, a German who had not long ago returned from South America. His father, who had been high up in the German army, had taken the family there at the end of World War II.

Germans owned a lot of firms and factories in Argentina. They were playing a waiting game.

—We have to support the Arabs, he told Mick, who spoke very little German. Hold my belt, he said, and then he took a crap in a Haare bus shelter.

—Now follow me, but keep your distance. We'll ask the priest, he'll give us 10 euros for beer.

Every one around knew that he was a Nazi, but the priest still gave him charity.

The Arabs' battle for their native land, the Arab's battle for their property— it's remarkable, is it not? Yes. It's remarkable.

At the end of World War II I had a chance to feel like Mozart. The Germans were trying to rescue 100 cows from the Königsberg region that the Russians had just occupied. They were mooing in pain because they had too much milk. My sister and I had to milk them all, even though there was nowhere to put the milk. That's when I felt like Mozart.

Just yesterday I witnessed a sparring match between the two 'gentlemen of cape and sword': Paul McCartney again defeated Mick Jagger in fencing.

Great work, when you know that it will still be meaningful 3,000 years from now. It was Jagger's idea. That's the way he lives.

Annette, with true inner peace and romanticism, though the same way.

I could write about 10 other occasions when Paul McCartney's thoughts about people and objects around them coincided perfectly. But I won't enumerate them. Your servant [who writes this] has a conscience that insists on accurate recording of the facts.

After the fencing we went to the park. Inexplicable melancholy: a bandage, sadly torn; the shade of a pine tree, a dragonfly, a gentle breeze—a crushed, sad heart. In the struggle for what is good, we sometimes get sad, and we start to feel sorry, ultimately feeling sorry for ourselves. The beauty of ambition is fanatically deep. There is more truth in the name 'Perkūnas' than in the name 'Christ'. Rolling stones. Rolling Stones.

Arabs are not savages, they know hospitality. They obey the code of honour even when it is not useful for them. I can boldly say: 'Wonderful!' An altruist's love is like a free queen in chess. Whereas, for example, when the German is in love he remains an egoist. For him, love is so holy that it ends up being of no benefit either to himself or his opposite party. For a German, love is for particularly tough people.

76

Arabs strike at Christians' hearts with their ultimate sacrifice: suicide missions.

These scenes need to be analysed and evaluated in a non-trite way. They are dedicated, but their mistake is that they do not have the time to create adequate movements and armies to protect their interests. Their second mistake is lack of unity. The first—haste; second—internal disagreements.

As I write these words to you, my kitten, Praha, is purring on my knees.

It is tedious, searching for wonderment. But I find it. It is better than smoking grass. The success of our efforts is when we notice something wonderful.

Why are there Muslim suicide-bombers? For themselves (this is a planning error), for their family, for their nation, and for humanity, which livens up when searching for the ringing mobile, wanting to say: oh yes, oh yes, but is that what you want? You have to fight with niceness; and after putting in 300 billion worth of niceness for the means, the education, the ideology—then we can ask: "Is that what you want?" Oh yes, oh yes, they will all say. Because with niceness, any evil can be conquered. Otherwise there would be no love, either. There would just be rapes and people taking a number at the counter to get married. I would like the gentlemen to deal with this idea.

Socialism was swept away because the people fancied capitalism more. A vision of across the river under the shade of the trees. Muslims fancy paradise more, where Allah sits.

Every year the USA wastes 300 billion on its army. If it were to dedicate that money to education, to an ideology of love, or the Good Reputation and Code of Honour category, the results would be different. Differences of world view, barriers between different national governments, pride, a desire to dominate: these are things that need to be overcome by journalists and artists—or with the help of politicians and sums allocated by them, for example 300 million dollars. It is a mistake to think that if you are boss, I must be dumb; or that if I am boss, then you must be dumb.

Jagger is talented in a choleric 'spit-catch' sort of way; therefore you can expect that he will be successful in all his endeavours, as long as they are something that is still going to be meaningful 3,000 years from now.

I'm a Nazi. Georgia, Georgia *über alles*. I'm not the only one. It gets better: the Georgian woman is pregnant. Bloody hell, the Georgians are being exterminated!

Way back, when I knew nothing about nail fungus, way back, when the barbarians from Homer's era lost so many positions, right up to the present, how many ice-age cannibals (up to Homer's time, and then and now)... Progress was determined by Christianity. So, let it correct our Code of Honour into the future.

Reputations can be regained. Maybe it's the same for the Arabs Muslims, and here they need help from us, the Christians. We need to unite Islam and Christianity. To stop the tragic tremors afflicting the student hostel we call Earth. In Córdoba, Spain, where in the 5th century there were many bathhouses

77

and libraries, there is still a mosque—under the same roof with the Catholic Cathedral.

Memories.

Only two or three times did Mick have a real sleep for an hour or two, when he found a car unlocked. He used to snooze in the city bus at night too, until it reached its destination in the suburbs.

"You toad!" is the worst native Lithuanian swearword; the sort of thing you would hear in the Caritas soup kitchen, when the retarded fellow is playing his accordion, and his cross-eyed old mum, no less crazy than him, is singing, what a cute family portrait—this is when someone says "You toads!"

You get into the student hostel, you lash out with your hands and feet, you pummel the baddy, you blow up the error-makers right in the middle of hatching their plan, you get good vibes in the meaningfulness department, the beauty department, the Code of Honour department and you achieve victory—wonderful! That is the meaning of life for us old rockers.

Arabs go across the student hostel courtyard and feel the Americans' lewd stares. They are undressing them with their eyes and fondling them in all sorts of ways. This is how the Arab–Jewish conflict appears.

I am a sex bomb, a professor in the people's university, says Annette. My breasts and my backside—they are serious motivators. Your petroleum and your silliness—that's what motivates the Americans. What's crazy are these suicide missions: it's number 28's turn today.

Nothing in life is so important as a good name. The examples of practitioners of karate, kamikaze and Muslim martyrs show, that pain is not a terrible thing. What's terrible is a bad reputation. It is my mission to make known the Muslims' Code of Honour and to suggest attractive methods of improving it.

One third of people are unclean. How to be safe from them? For this purpose a Ministry is needed with an annual budget of 300 billion dollars and capable administrators. This was what was talked about in relation to Good Reputation.

The partisan method of warfare, buying Satan with spare cash (it's he that will have to stand trial in God's court, not you), allowable/non-allowable method of warfare with the baddies—that's the hope!

Čiurlionis! We take a sample from that which we call a pure soul, dignity. An answer is spat out by my computer, the gold of my black box: such dignity, it's wonderful!

The pain of love.

Mick was making every effort to get to know Annette better, because he truly esteemed the idea of true love.

When he was in Milan, after a phone call to Annette, Mick went up to the top level of the railway station and was thinking of jumping off, because he was suffering incredibly, knowing that Paul was with Annette while she was on the phone. They were sharing a pizza together. And what were they going to do after that?

Follow good example. Style is for both the peasant and the king.

If Hemmingway had been not a fisherman, but a public toilet attendant, he would have bequeathed us not "The Old Man and the Sea", but "The Immigrant and the Shit Factory". But we do not notice any light-hearted humour around while a Caesarean section operation is taking place.

The maximum dignity is the march through history of the old rockers who believe profoundly in their own talents and their money. They make some fine efforts. Good luck to us: cheers, setbacks—sympathy from numerous sympathisers.

Let the Japanese Hiroshima survivor tell us whether love is flourishing in our student hostel. Yes, the Japanese would say. If there were no love, I would miss it.

Sean put up with the Mecca heat with me, and it was OK with him. Travel—full of mini dramas, the last of which—nightmarish.

Unselfish dignity moves one to tears. At Haare, Munich, Rod Stewart, David Bowie, Mick Jagger, Charlie Watts and Paul McCartney don white lab jackets and visit Dr Zurab Mšvidobadze. They are following his project and they believe in him. By coincidence, Annette's connections were what determined success for Dr Mšvidobadze's laboratory.

—I'm essentially a Franciscan, said Mšvidobadze.

—We're essentially Franciscans, too, said Jagger. Gates agreed.

Right up until the Renaissance Arab culture and Islam had a clear cultural, scientific and technological advantage over Western Europe.

For Jagger, Islam smelled sometimes of plums, sometimes of blackberries. He felt a precise feeling: a patient's fear of the dentist—a fear that you are exactly as you are, nothing more.

—Are we drinking again today? asked a longhair with a hundred questions.

—What? the Rolling Stones' drummer wanted to know precisely. Something with a name?

—Answer straight away, said Jagger.

—Straight away, said Watts, if not sooner. My hand shakes, it's hard to hold the bottle to my lips.

—Go to the petrol station, said Jagger. He had a bruise under his eye, as red as a new fire engine, but he couldn't remember who had given it to him. I would go myself, but my muscles have become unreliable, as if I had spent the last two years in a shed on the Liverpool base.

A fragrant summer night, the young nun gave her vows, an early Arabic morning was dawning.

79

They had been beating their breasts about not drinking any more, but this morning the thought that had infiltrated their minds was: booze.

—I think Watts wants it, not us. We don't need it, said Jagger. So he and Rod Stewart, like good little choirboys, bought only champagne, no hard stuff.

Watts bought some wine.

—You won't be having any wine, said Watts.

—Oh yes we will, replied Jagger.

—The Phantom is following behind, announced Watts.

After some time Rod Stewart said:

—The Phantom will be at the petrol station.

Who is the Phantom? It turns out to be Annette, keeping an eye on the boozers. Grown-up adults playing the Phantom.

About: sleep.

Mick woke up in his railway wagon on the way to the Italian coast. No people around. He went through all the carriages—empty. The engine driver's chair was also empty. The train was standing in a siding. Empty. The doors were locked, so he climbed out a window. He slept for a while in the grass by the tracks and got on board another train, this one bound for Rome. As luck would have it, the ticket inspector was a nasty number; he punched Mick about and booted him off the train.

These days there are many misunderstandings based on emotions. The chador has been banned from French schools. That is a form of discrimination. The Islamo-fascists, which is how they should be called, have a tried and true weapon: fear. The concept of Jihad goes against God's nature and against common sense.

Rod Stewart phoned the water supply department in Mecca on 545–224. They supplied some alcohol too. The people risked their lives.

Allah's messenger said: "Do not believe until you have reached the point where you want for your brother the same that you want for yourself".

By the way, Jews were banned from going to Mecca.

"Allah is Holy and Great, and his gift is the gardens of Paradise".

The rockers had a tourist visa, they did not get a Hajj visa. Our offering was five years worth of Goodness Coupons, a two year old cow and a one year old sheep or goat with no imperfections.

Between the two hills of As-Safa and Al-Marwah in Mecca, there is a covered two storey gallery 395 metres long and 20 metres wide. One does a ritual walk between them in honour of Abraham's wife.

Good places for prayer are:

1) the *al-multa zama* (between the doors of the Kaaba and the black stone)

2) 20 metres either side of the spring

3) on the As-Safa hill

4) by the big pole and smaller poles.

The crowd is like a refugee camp of 200 huge tents. It is essential to throw stones at the *jamarat* and to give alms. This was determined by Abraham. Allah sent the Black Rock together with Adam. All through the centuries Mecca has been closed to non-Muslims. And only the good graces of Cat Stevens enabled the rockers to blend in with the masses of thousands of pilgrims.

Holy places in Mecca:

1) Minas plains
2) al-Chaif mosque
3) Arafat plains
4) Namire mosque
5) Murdolif plains
6) Prophet's House
7) Mount Chiro and cliff
8) al-Malia cemetery
9) Mosque of the Djinns
10) Ibn al-Walid Mosque
11) al-Kura University

The Religious Police looked after the rockers and helped them in every way.

The Hajj is a complicated ritual, requiring physical, spiritual and intellectual preparation.

—Do you remember how I was annoying you at Rome airport? Jagger asked Watts. Nail fungus is a laugh compared to 50°C. heat.

—Saudi Arabia has reserves of 39.5 billion tons of petroleum, said Watts. I keep wondering how to get my hands on some of it.

—You were always as ambitious as the cowherd of the cow Žalioji, the calf Bukis and the heifer Iva, said Jagger, in a voice with about as much warmth as the ice cubes rattling around in the bar. Willy–nilly, in his thoughts he always came back to Bar X.

—1.5 billion people practice Islam, observed Cat Stevens. Russia has an advantage: there are 20 million Muslims in Russia.

—Gee I need a drink, Rod Stewart complained.

—Even brandy, I'll descend to that.

—One of the biggest deserts in the world, Rub al-Khali, is in Saudi Arabia, so it's not surprising that you're thirsty, said Watts.

Jagger feels his bruise and nods his head.

—"There is no God but Allah", repeated Cat Steven three times. "B'ismi 'l-lah!" (In the name of God.) "Al-lahu akbar!" (God is great.)

'Tawaf' means walking seven times around the Kaaba in an anti-clockwise direction. They kiss the black stone three times.

There were some problems. There is only one petrol station on the Sharurah–Najran Highway, about halfway along. Sand carries about 30 metres a year. There is about 2.5 millimetres of rain per year. Hyenas, jackals, rodents, sand gazelles and plenty of snakes.

The Hajj was instituted by Abraham. A woman is accompanied by her husband or a male relative, in Annette's case—Cat Stevens. Blood and milk.

The primary invocation of the Hajj is the 'talbiyah': "Here I am, O God, at Thy Command! Here I am at Thy Command! Thou art without associate; here I am at Thy Command! Thine are praise and grace and dominion! Thou art without associate."

Memories.

In a Japanese restaurant, Mick drank some *saké*, pawning his Rolex, which the head waiter thought was a Chinese fake. He told Annette by telephone:

—If I don't find somewhere to have a wash and sleep tonight, I'm going to kill myself. This type of suffering is too much for me to bear.

***

Address by Bill Gates, Jonas Mekas, Mick Jagger and Charlie Watts to a United Nations session on Arab–Jewish relations.

***

(written by Jurga Ivanauskaitė)

—Gentlemen, said Mick Jagger, from the podium of the United Nations assembly. There are millions of musicians, but the Beatles and the Rolling Stones are at the top. Using our heads we looked at the problem of emigration, and no one had to wait long to see the results of our work. This is borne out by last year's statistics. Now we have turned our attention to the Arab–Jewish problem, and we are sure that we will achieve more than corrupt politicians, who are also hampered by legislation. Charlie Watts told me: we will crack that nut, all we need is some suitcases filled with 200 billion dollars. That is the principle of a conscientious worker, who does not work for free. The Jewish crooks and their cronies have got designs on the oil reserves of Iraq, Iran, Saudi Arabia and they are creating strategies to gain control of it. For some reason the USA is not using its own oil reserves. That's the tip of the iceberg for you. The Arabs need to unite, and the Western world needs to be humanists and chase the pro–Jewish politicians out of their positions of power. First—'educating' the Arabs and sweet talking them. Second—magnanimity from the Western world. Perkūnas is severe, but just. His rolling stones will crush and put back in their place any that foul the air because of their natural inclination to fart.

I will tell you what we did in Mecca. Pilgrims giving alms follow the Prophet's example by shaving off or cutting their hair. Pilgrims may shave their head more than once over the hajj, but they do not touch their beard or whiskers. It is not permitted to use perfume, to pluck grass, to cut down trees, to wear anything other than properly sewn clothes, or to have sexual intercourse.

A column of thousands of worshippers visits the holy places. Perspiration flows in streams. It is very hot. My pride was affected. Can an Arab outdo a Brit in any way? I sensed their fanatical belief and pride in their culture. It was amazing. A true, unfeigned fascination and romanticism. Looking at it from a vantage point of thousands of years you see a corpus of remarkable fantasy, beauty and elements to be marvelled at, which are passed down from generation to generation, because no one has thought of anything better up to now. I would like to see British lecturers at Medina's Islamic university, where there is a Faculty of Islamic and Holy Qur'an Studies and a Faculty of the Arabic language, and I would like there to be a Christian Fellowship associated with the Faculty of Islamic and Holy Qur'an Studies.

That is why I request 200 billion dollars in funding from the UN, which we, the old rockers, will use for education: for the creation and propagation of a humanist ideology.

In Vietnam the Russians flew holding their eyes open with their fingers, and therefore so many got shot down, because they had pedal controls for the planes.

In Mecca the Jews disguised themselves as Arabs and they caused them such trouble, that we in the West went frantic.

Just imagine, a column of thousands, and here comes a greeting from Auntie. Five swarms of bees, all hybridised with African bees, killer bees, released from cotton bags, a thousand in each swarm, attacking the pilgrims. We, the Brits, were witnesses, and we 'engaged reverse gear'. That helped us out. The lad from his granny's moonshine still can tell you the rest.

Charlie Watts replaced Mick Jagger on the podium, feeling up the audience with his eyes, as if wanting to check whether the torch of human kindness was still flickering.

***

Item: Look what people are like!

Mick and Charlie were sitting by a pedestrian bridge in Rome. Mick was showing his bare, bleeding leg with the big toenail torn off. Over several hours, the amount of alms they collected was: nil.

***

— Gentlemen and lady! We are eternally indebted to humanity, whatever you say, yes, we are. We have to make an effort on behalf of future generations, we have to make sacrifices in the name of altruism, like generations have done before us, and today we are enjoying the fruits of the largesse they created.

The sincerity of the two old rockers is larger-than-life. They ask to be trusted explicitly.

—Because we are, together with hell's angels, working to restore order, and it doesn't matter whether we are saints or sinners. What's important is that we

83

do the job (yes, a paid job, that's true; but we do it out of non-self-interested principle). I can see you all smiling so much that the U.N. building is all lit up, and your eyes are shining so much that if you looked in a mirror you would shout in horror. Dear citizens... is it OK that I call you citizens? I see that some delegates have had some German beer. And why not? It's we, the Rolling Stones who are risking our lives, not they. Is this that same idea, for which we forget about the whole world

Our experience is our apparel, Friedrich Nietzsche said. And we old rockers seek and find the experience that brings ideas, because lightning doesn't ask where to strike. Perkūnas and the Rolling Stones say to you: we carry revolution around like a referee carries a whistle on a string. But there are no letters. You say, my sad citizen, that a hawk flew off with the encoder? We, the knights of cape and sword, ask for just 200 billion to establish the Empire of Art, because the USA's annual budget for military matters is 300 billion. Just think, you save a hundred billion, and the job gets done by the most capable people on Earth. A country is the biggest and richest real estate firm. We request 10,000 buildings in Druskininkai, Lithuania, or Yalta, Ukraine. Let's vote for it!

Our security guard is the Yellow Brigades. Get them mad and they'll thump you, and for a thousand—they'll lay you out, whereas for two thousand—dead and buried in the flower beds opposite the White House, without Presidential approval. Let's vote!—said Charlie Watts.

Just two hands went up—the Lithuanian delegate and the Ukrainian delegate. Clearly, there were not enough votes.

—Well, gentleman, continued Charlie Watts. We don't get money by being nice. Just feel what we felt in Mecca. A biological weapon —killer bees. After being stung by them a person gets ill with paranoia. The Arabs caught a lot of those bees with nets and in the future they will use them against the Americans. A General, sick with paranoia, will send an atomic missile into the White House and the third world war will start.

Well, I can see you are as unmoved as those 25 kg weights somebody left in the corner of the hall. Therefore the two of us are going to perform a gangbang using all sorts of means, and no exceptions for flu or periods. *En garde*, here we come!

Outside the window of the U.N. it was raining. The rain was tapping on the glass like the felt-tip paws of a kitten when Watts opened a bag and let a swarm of bees loose. These attacked people, who ran around like crazy, trying to hide under tables. The imprint left by this horror was justified, like Perkūnas' rolling stones.

—Attention, gentlemen, Watts said after a pause. The sting of these bees is not dangerous, it even helps ease rheumatism. But we have a swarm of genetically modified bees in another bag. So let's vote again: who is in favour of giving us old rockers 200 billion dollars for our mission to found the Empire of Art?

The U.N. assembly hall was suddenly a sea of upraised hands as people unanimously supported the Rolling Stones' proposal.

84

Jonas Mekas' film about himself, which was the last word in horror movie technology, convinced the politicians that evil can rear its ugly head anywhere.

—Gentlemen, said Jagger, replacing Watts, that aristocratic creature, you have all had a fright. That was a bluff. Only the Russian delegation didn't scare easily. The Yellow Brigades have information that in Brazil the Russians have a laboratory spreading the killer bees. They have an antidote—we don't. We must take account of that in our plans. Private initiative is always more effective than public. It's precisely for that reason that socialism failed.

Annette.

Jagger found out a little about Annette's tastes when there was a film about Turkish immigrants showing in Haare. Annette and Paul walked out after a few episodes.

Jagger liked it. That's the way he behaved himself, setting a low standard within a few minutes. The film was being shown in the café at Haare.

***

(written by Jurga Ivanauskaitė, a Lithuanian)

Campfire, gallows, and Russian-speaking Grim Reaper holding a swarm of bees with 50 drones, three queens and 10,000 worker bees.

Keith Richards said:

—Rembrandt is no Jagger, so we have to listen to Jagger's music. Tell me, young lady, have I succeeded in frightening you? The crowd and the milling pilgrims—the great work of Mekas in Mecca. And what about the terrible stinging of the bees, after which you lose your mind, and the third world war starts? Impressed?

—Oh, yes, I'm impressed, said the girl. What's really impressive is the rockers' superiority over Putin, Bush and Blair.

***

Love quadrilateral. P. McCartney

The sun shuffles along in its golden sandals. The winged orchestra of the forest grove is playing an *adagio*. The young grass around the edges of the forests is destined for the hay-drying racks. For pitching the hay three-prong or four-prong pitchforks are great.

But Paul McCartney, a warrior, he manages a bass guitar better than a pitchfork. In a certain year he achieved recognition as world's best bass guitarist. Not to mention, that he's not a bad composer, maybe one of the best. No one is better than him at talking to soothe you when you need a splinter or a tooth removed. Paul is gentle, he enchants you, and his intonations inspire trust.

His dealings with women and children are something special. He has found his love in the details, creating a unique aura, in which his opponents feel conveniently safe.

The Culture Department, which he headed, required particular forms and correct decisions. Every morning he would get up and compose two songs. He already has a couple of hundred, and after a year he will choose the very best of them and then he will produce an album called "And what will you reply, John?"

The government of Germany donated the Munich suburb of Haare for the Empire of Art project. It was a large tract of land with one hundred buildings. In years gone by, right from the time of King Ludwig, the area had been used for psychiatric hospital buildings. The highest building was seven storeys high. The property was signed over to P. McCartney, M. Jagger and A. Hess, with no right to sell the property. The Empire's ruler—fuehrer—was Annette Hess.

Druskininkai, Raushen and Yalta had also been offered, but thanks to Annette's authority, Haare had been obtained under favourable conditions. These included all that one needed to live there: rest home and hospital style buildings with two-person wards, and a convenient catering system (there was a central kitchen that supplied all the buildings). Rock stars are fairly pampered, so the menu was prepared a week in advance.

Paul slept in one ward with Annette. He was sentimentally attached to John Lennon's son. He loved him. Sean slept alone. Paul was a workaholic. He couldn't stand being without work for even a minute. The psychiatric patients had not all moved out yet, and the rockers were having encounters with people being treated for addiction to alcohol and narcotics, and for paranoia.

Initially, for the next five years, the Empire of Art will have four administrative departments: the Department of Art and Culture, the Department of Emigration, the Department of Arabic Affairs (the 'Arab arabesque'), and the Military Department, the latter being dedicated entirely to pacifist activity.

Paul bought some art works, a couple of canvases each of Cézanne, Modigliani, van Gogh (John Lennon loved him very much), Matisse and Chagall. These were meant to inspire feeling in the artists: idealisations of scenes from the life of simple people.

Today, for example, Paul put a tick in the professionalism box, and he wrote two songs (the *minimum* for someone at the General's level). He was also a General in the meals, clothes, and sleep category (he was fasting and went without sleep twice a week, because Mick Jagger had told him that he had raised his own intellectual level this way). And in the good reputation category, there were his efforts to recruit a writer, a Dane, to write a novel containing the word 'wonderful' on every page. McCartney agreed with Annette. The word 'wonderful' is a narcotic that gives a pleasant and non-dangerous buzz—it is the incarnation of happiness.

Paul talked with the Dane about Cézanne's painting 'Maison au toit rouge' (*'House with a red roof'*), a subtle evocation of exciting detail; Chagall's 'L'anniversaire' (*'The Birthday'*), which has fantasy accessible to all; Kurbe's

86

'Nature morte' (*'Still Life'*), which idealises details of everyday life; and Degas'
'Buveur d'absinthe' (*'The absinthe drinker'*), happiness for a few euros.

Paul was working. He read several chapters of the Dane's novel and gave some instructions.

In the category of love, friendship and sympathy (Ringo Starr's Mental Technique) was his engagement to Annette. All the rocker élite envied him. Annette was a super girl, with Rudolph Hess' hard brains, which telegrammed exotica to all who gazed upon her.

—Paul, said Annette, what questions were you studying today?

—It's difficult with the Danish author, said Paul, and with the Arab painter. But we are hopeful. The Centre Pompidou has ordered the Arab's canvas. Everything is going according to plan.

—Today Mick and I are going to the bank, Annette told Paul.

—It's cold outside, put on your warm underwear, Paul responded.

—Really? asked Annette, doubtfully.

Paul was so envious of Mick that he wanted Annette to wear heavy underwear, so that she would be embarrassed if Jagger tried to undress her.

—Really, replied Paul the Crafty.

—So when is the fencing? asked Annette. Today Mick is giving a lecture to Ringo Starr's Mental Technique sect members in Brussels. He needs to take two flights to return tomorrow to Munich, to Haare.

—Today I won't be fencing. I'm fasting. It's my second night without sleep; I'm cleansing my body of toxins. I feel that I'm going to get back the form I had in 1964–1965.

—My kitten is spitting blood, said Annette. My kitten, Praha.

—I'll take him to the vet, said Paul. Please accept a present: Max Ernst's painting *"Brook near Leipzig"*. Modernists will help us to learn to say the word 'wonderful'. And when things really are wonderful—you are happy.

—The Danish author, said Annette, puts in too much cheap humour. For example, he makes fun of the way immigrants speak: *"Vot's* up? *Vot* did you say? *Vot* happened? Okay, *ve'll* let *dis* one in, his mouth is big enough to hold a double burger". And so forth. Cheap humour doesn't win the reader's heart. Writers are a nasty breed. They write with such feeling, as if they were driving the last spike of the transcontinental railway. I am all for a laconic, simple, diplomatic style, à la Maupassant. Cheap humour is OK among people you know well. Not in a novel. The Dane is as gullible as Jean Marais in the role of the Count. Good. Now Indian file, off to work, choo choo, like making a train in kindergarten. You, Paul, to the grand piano, I'll go and talk to Sean. He's a remarkable lad. That's what good genes mean.

***

87

Department of Pacifism

Love Quadrilateral—by Lennon the Elder. A fine landscape. Two houses with Yellow Brigade protection. The Yellow Brigades are a 'Hells Angels' type security force composed of Japanese, which Yoko Ono put together for Sean.

—How is Handke? Annette asked Zurab.

—Peter would like to be dreaming, wandering around the forest gathering lily of the valley flowers, that's his nature.

But in fact he's in the garage, drinking schnapps with a metalworker—said Zurab.

—Looks like the bee-stings affected him so much that he has suffered a breakdown in the Hedonism category. That's all he lives for now. He told me he's smoking hashish.

—Could be. From my chat with him, I suspect that he is sliding into paranoia. He is having trouble in the Fantasy, Imagination, Beauty categories. He reads too much meaning into his environment and he has built a fantasy castle on false assumptions; if the foundations could be destroyed that castle would collapse and he would get better.

—But we are the guilty ones, said Annette. We invited him to participate in this experiment.

—Let's go get Sean, said the Japanese that Yoko Ono had chosen for Sean. Sort of like the Swiss Guards at the Vatican.

Those two buildings have 50 beds, two to a room. It's the Military Pacifist Department, which Sean is in charge of.

—What is Peter Handke's condition? Annette asks a Japanese who was on his way back from the Arts Department.

Item: Envy

Breakfast at Haare is at 8 am. In the cafeteria the first table is for Paul and Annette. Mick decided not to give up. He sat down beside Annette and offered her some French cheese. She doted on Paul, like a good housekeeper, a good friend, and, well... if you like... a good lover. Exasperated, Mick picked up a glass and threw it against the wall.

Annette was aroused by Mick's ardour.

—Peter Henke is Joan of Arc. He is saintly, said a member of the Yellow Brigade.

—How many bees did you manage to catch and bring from Brazil? Annette asked one of the Japanese.

—A couple of hundred. They are breeding now and we are interrogating them.

—Are there any killer bees among them?

—No. Jagger conned the U.N. Although—who can tell for sure... ?

Annette went up to the second floor, where Zurab Mšvidobadze was working in his laboratory.

Zurab Mšvidobadze:

—This week we'll have a new medicine, and maybe it will cure Handke. The laboratory works with selected patients according to the principles of subconscious activity. Handke is convinced that he is John Kennedy's son. But what is at the root of his ravings, we don't know yet. Sean is now testing the bees, whose venom contains the chemical that causes paranoia.

—I'll go upstairs to where he is, said Annette. She left the invalid scooter, in which she had driven over from the group of buildings that housed the Arts Department. There were about thirty such groups of buildings at Haare. Two thirds of the real patients had left. Those that remained were volunteers participating in the experiment, who were almost cured.

So Annette, with her puffed-out dress and her two remarkable faces, looked like an enigma, and Sean became serious upon seeing her. He could not admit to himself that he was in love with Annette. He upheld the principle of "Thou shalt not covet another's woman". Annette was Paul McCartney's fiancée. For half a year already. All that time Sean had been struggling with his feelings, however he did not intend to make any advance on the super-beauty.

—Sean, Annette said when she reached the second story, I've been helping the German and English authors. We are writing novels about the secrets of biological weapons. That should put a stop to the arms race. The media are the only front on which to combat the politicians, who base all they do on the principles of brute force.

—Your Highness... began Sean.

—Don't call me that! I am Annette.

—You are the fuehrer of our Empire, I need to observe protocol.

—We are priests without cassocks, said Annette. We are philanthropists, doing common battle for happiness, and all that is good. What do you say to that?

***

Before answering, Sean reflected on how in Haare there was this young Jewess, an Interpol agent, who had fallen in love with Mick. She was being treated for drug dependency.

In the cafeteria Mick was telling her how an Interpol officer initiates a new starter into the job. He gives him a nail and tells him to hammer it into the wall using his forehead as a hammer. The newcomer tries, but the nail bends. He goes to check the other side of the wall and finds that the reason for the nail bending was that there was a policeman sleeping with his head up against the wall where the nail was supposed to come through!

Mick and the Jewess were having a good chuckle, which Annette noticed—not with indifference, it must be said.

89

***

—I will say, replied Sean, that happiness is seeing you and being reminded that you are unique, physically and spiritually; in other words—awesome.

—Wait, wait, said Annette. What will we do to ensure that there are no more victim-volunteers like Peter Handke? He volunteered for this experiment because he thinks that this would be a more useful humanitarian effort than writing novels. Our loved ones are going to early graves while we just picnic in the orchards. When I think about Peter, my soul crackles, as if a high-tension power line had fallen on me.

—When I come out into the *dojo*, said Sean, I am ready for victory or death. Likewise with the medicine that Zurab Mšvidobadze's team is trialling next week. I believe in them. That medicine will be as fine as poetry. And also... your fine humour and gentle concern, oh noble Annette, capture the heart of all who have dealings with you.

—Don't be so formal, said Annette.

—Well, said Sean, I don't dare to be too familiar. I don't want to poke a stick in Paul's spokes. And when is Mick Jagger coming back?

—Jagger? Tomorrow. Now he's one who likes a joke. He told me that my make-up looks as if I had done it by feel in the dark and with dislocated hands.

—Uncle Mick, said Sean, is a fine singer. He is like my dad in some ways. The same aggression of someone attacking in a battle for truth and love. Jagger is tough. So tough, it's amazing.

—What is really amazing, said Annette is that Mr Perkūnas / Rolling Stones always has an eye on the nice señoras—and their grubby mates. Always ladies in his life, always new ones.

—You have some affection for him? asked Sean.

—I believe that three people can love each other at once.

—And which three would they be?

—Well, Paul, my fiancée; Mick, the world's sex bomb; and Sean, family friend. My greatest goal, apart from the concerns of the Empire, would be to have a son, although a daughter would be nice too. I tremble thinking about it. I saw a Venezuelan film, in which the pedestrian pavement was roped off, and as the hero went over it, the ropes trembled as if they had been smoking hashish. Art and life should be amazing even without LSD—without Lucy in the Sky.

—Are you sincere?

—Well, think about it, am I joking, or am I getting it all off my chest and telling the truth? The blues of rhythm, with a nasty motive: tears or erection?

***

How did Annette buy off Mick? With her smile. A polite, distancing smile. The Bessie Smith method. A smile within the bounds of politeness. That's style. And style enchanted Mick.

90

Mick told her how once he had been sleeping in a railway sleeper factory on stacks of wood. The boss chased him off, wouldn't let him sleep. What harm was he doing? Just sleeping. But the world hates bums and doesn't feel sorry for them.

Mick is telling Annette how one time a girl in Florida, a German, invited to pay his fare for him to sail across the Atlantic with her on a liner. But his pride got in the way.

***

Emigration Department
Love rectangle—Jagger

(written by Jurga Ivanauskaitė)

In the lift at Haare, Mick was kissing the Jewess from Interpol. She was resisting, but they still went to bed at Paul's place. Annette was away dealing with the Arabic issue.

The Jewess took revenge on Mick big time for not valuing her and not giving her what she wanted from him.

It reminded Mick of the unhappiest day of his life, when his friends made fun of him on the football field, gently and subtly, but he went away blubbering and some passer-by asked him: "What have some meanies done to you, young fellow?", and he cried even more bitterly.

***

Item: history, plus feeling, plus victory by the sapience of feeling. A certain meditational system.

***

—Uncle Mick, said Sean. The Yellow Brigades have supplied some surveillance film from Brazil, which shows Ivan Ivanovich Ivanov smuggling a cotton bag full of bees out of the apiary. He did the same thing that we did.

—Even baddies can get ideas from Ringo Starr's Mental Technique, replied Uncle Mick Jagger. No doubt they have learned something from our bluff at the U.N., and if they try something, it's 100% likely that the White House will be attacked by paranoid Generals. War in the hands of half-wits. Knight's turn to advance.

—What can we do to counter that? asked Sean.

—We have to catch Ivan Ivanovich Ivanov and poke out his eye.

—And will you do that?

—If you don't eat the wolf, the wolf will eat you, said Jagger.

91

Now we are getting scientific ideas not only from bees, but also from ants, which can also be used as a biological weapon. Zurab Mšvidobadze is a General among scientists. We must warn the Yellow Brigades of the possibility that some Ivan Ivanov may come with millions of them in a duffle bag and may try to use them for evil purposes.

—The Russians, said Jagger, are a bit more than a fly's fart. In military systems, they are at about Mozart level. Capable and persistent. I am convinced that bees and psychiatric illnesses are both something foisted on the world by Russians. That's their Little Serenade. These days an atomic weapon is just a pistol, but bees, well... they are a terror-causing unknown quantity.

—How are the emigration problems going? asked Sean.

—Just imagine a 112 kg gangster with an expression that says he's always ready to dive into the raging sea to earn a bottle of vodka. That's how members of the *Ku-Klux Klan* look to poor immigrants from underdeveloped countries. Or else imagine a Jew who uses his Masonic contacts to milk half the world, even though he's an immigrant. There are many problems. But we are dealing with them.

—I hesitate to ask, but...

—Ask, my boy. You are like a son to me.

—Do you feel something for Annette beyond your civic responsibility and humanitarian aims?

—You know, replied Mick, I could love her, even if I found out she were the Nazi's godmother. I could love her, without hardly seeing her face. But... But I would really love her because she is a Siamese twin. I could name nine reasons why I don't like Paul. And they would all be because of Annette, whom, I have observed, you gaze upon with trembling delight.

For Annette's birthday, Mick gave her some of the best cigarillos. She thanked him and said:

—Paul has made a reservation for him and me at a café tonight; I'll be there with Paul this evening. I hope you have nothing against Paul.

—Yes, yes, said Mick Jagger, biting his tongue.

Arab Department

When you get out of the metro train, you go two kilometres along a road that is a bus route, and there the first buildings of the Empire of Art begin. At that point there is a checkpoint attended by the Yellow Brigade, which protects this Lilliputian country. There the city-state starts—on the site of a former psychiatric clinic. The Administration of the Empire of Art established the Empire right there, where Annette had served time for the Nazi passages in her novel. That sentence was a joke. She liked Haare so much, and its Alcohol and Drug Dependency Section, in which she served her sentence, that she suggested the Empire of Art be established there, and she got all the necessary paperwork done in half a year. Over that time most of the patients moved out, only a few remained.

Five billionaires became the owners of Haare: Bill Gates, Annette Hess, Paul McCartney, Mick Jagger and Sean Lennon. Money was of interest to them to the extent that their characters had been formed by capitalist fiscal communism.

***

Memories.

With his bike he crawled into some sort of scrub, not far from the Munich Olympic Village, and since the day and night were warm, he slept on the ground, having not yet experienced a bladder infection, which he feared very much.

***

Cat Stevens was in charge of the Arabic Department. It was decided that it should operate for the next five years, then if necessary, another five. And so forth.

Cat Stevens, who adopted Islam long ago, was a negotiator in the deliberations on education in the Islamic countries.

—How's it going for your pair of authors working on an Islamic best seller? Annette asked Cat Stevens. I would like to suggest that the main hero be an Arab born in Germany. After careful thought I say: if you want to be happy—go ahead. Get your buzz from all that is "wonderful". What's wonderful is wonderful. For the first sentence, which is very very important, I offer the Arabic novelists the following: "The June morning carried its head on a plate".

—Would you like some hot chocolate, asked the brunette with the friendly gap in her chequered pantyhose? Yes? OK, I'll bring some. But maybe take off your jacket? At least initially, for a trial period?

—I took it off. I am as bare as brass, said a bluenose who appeared out of nowhere. Maybe you could lend me a crappy euro... And so on and so forth.

—Arabs and Muslims do not have your sense of humour, said Cat Stevens.

—Oh venerable bard, you have to grunt and sweat if you want to achieve something worthwhile.

—I will bring you a manuscript by an Arabic woman, which is unusual, but I think she is capable and we are translating her essay into German and English.

—And what about songs? Pop songs?

—Charlie Watts will write some lyrics for me, I've had so many dealings with him, said Cat Stevens. The great thing about oblivion is saying 'wonderful' to yourself. For example, Mick got quite upset that a sip of whiskey brought a tear to my eye. He drinks it like water. That's remarkable. I think we should use Sean instead. John Lennon: I can analyse him *ad nauseam* using scientific method. Sean can do ballads. People will buy them. Let's use Sean for

93

humanitarian purposes. He'll get some ideas from Jagger, who's in great form at the moment.

—Cat, I'll give you another sentence. You can use it for a song. "Autumn necrology. Toledo-style October chestnut gold minting."

***

Annette.

Annette has begun imitating the Jewess from Interpol with her funny pronunciation of the 'r' sound and in other ways. She also imitates Paul. He laughs and says he isn't in the slightest bit offended.

'A' for acting.

***

—Thank you, Annette, but even though Watts is a crook, he will give me better lyrics. For example, Sean has told me about Ivan Ivanovich Ivanov. Why not write some lyrics about him with a negative slant? Tee hee. Watts' trick with the bees at U.N. headquarters—that was a blast! And now here we are with our Empire of Art in place. Annette, go see the Pope, while it's still a German Pope. Another idea for you. It was suggested to me by an Arab musician. Mature poets love the truth even in cases where it appears simple, banal and naïve to the ordinary person. A community of standard conformist behaviour, that's cosy. It's easy, comfortable. And in a way—wonderful.

—Cat, maybe you have some doubts about my work style? As you know, 4–5 of us work on a novel together. One of us writes something about the 10 or so things we are focussing on, the next one adds some jokes, the third adds some dialogue; but it will all go out under my name only—Annette Hess. Because it's my idea. Just like, for example, the ashtray on the brass stand, the leather-bound walnut wood dishes, the chandelier of Czech crystal, my interlocutor clad in *Wrangler* jeans, the annoying flies buzzing around, the Munich radio playing Viennese pop favourites, same as all the other stations. Yes, the images: copies of *Playboy* and *Bild* magazines lying on the window sill, my interlocutor looking at me lustfully, as most men do, and I lavish him with passionate attention, just as I do with all men. It doesn't mean anything—it's simply just my style. My grandfather taught me what men value most: modesty and chastity. From my mother I learned humour, like this, for example, when I asked a private in the Yellow Guard :

—Where did that machine-gun come from? Looks like a Kalashnikov.

—I brought it from home, he replies.

—And where have you been all night?

—I was guarding the bridge.

—Who ordered you to do that? I asked him.

—Some major, they all look the same to me.

94

He was a hopeless alcoholic. But what do you love in others? The energy that I imbue them with. When I give a person about 50 of my ideas and jokes—that person automatically becomes dear and likable to me. And if I give him 100, then he either becomes my friend or my lover.

To win their sympathy, I shovel up a series of little crises. I smother the person in them. They are really a series of little love darts. They generate warmth, and modesty begets respect. Finally there are the character traits.

For example, John Lennon is very dear to me. He has a character that's a mixture of choler and melancholy. Those people immediately gain my liking.

—Like Jagger too? asked Cat Stevens.

—Yes. Like Jagger. Although I would prefer him with less choler and more melancholy.

—They say *Procol Harum* copied Bach, but I like them, because they are melancholics, said Stevens.

—Well I prefer *Free* and *Bad Company*. I like there melancholy, because melancholy is a non-self-interested feeling, a fragment of a small tragedy.

—I'm crushed. You like Jagger and McCartney better than me. Is it because of their creative successes/failures, or because of their manly charm?

—McCartney was more attractive than Alain Delon. Jagger is the Formula One of sex, a fireball, like one of those driven by Schuhmacher or that Austrian, the one who got burnt, what's his name? Oh yes, Nikki Lauda.

—If it weren't for your wheelchair, said Cat Stevens, you would be Miss Universe. I think you need to find an agent that will turn your minuses into pluses.

—Awesome, said Annette. I am truly something awesome.

Mick has walked all around the complex and he can't find Annette and Paul. They might be having a bath together, the thought occurs to him. But that is too painful for him to contemplate, so he lies down in a grumpy mood. He stretches out in the television room and suffers.

***

Memories.

Item: Happiness.

Mick, who has been drinking beer, lolls about in the sand embracing an Arab woman with a hairy upper lip—sun, sea, a true feeling of happiness.

***

Item: Happiness.

An exceptionally warm October. He is lying beside a river. The coolness of autumn, but with autumn sun, and the smell of autumn. Complete relaxation, complete happiness. He can smell the river.

***

Square

Annette was sleeping on the sixth floor, in a two-bed ward with Paul McCartney. Whether those two were doing anything, no one knows for sure. Jagger liked coming to Annette about work matters. (For example, in Block 11 a toilet flooded and wet the whole corridor.)

It so happened that Jagger, McCartney and Sean all brought Annette a little kitten each to replace the sick and exhausted one. She called them Praha2, Praha3 and Praha4. Annette was the happiest they had ever seen her. One day at lunch, McCartney tried to order a pizza in Lithuanian (in honour of the first time he had eaten pizza, baked by Jonas Mekas, at John Lennon's place). Two doves sat at the table and tasted Lithuanian pizza. Then Sean appeared, wanting to ask the fuehrer something. He wanted to share his happiness. Peter Handke was better or nearly better. He no longer thinks he is John Kennedy's son, nor the youngest son of God, Creator and Ruler of the Universe, and that Jesus Christ is a visitor from a far-away planet. Having weeded some quack grass, Peter was still a little fragile after his breakdown, but sanity was on its way back for him. Zurab Mšvidobadze patented some medicine that cures paranoia and the sting of those Brazilian bees, for which the antidote had been searched for so hard.

Annette sent a letter to various countries saying they could send their incurable patients, because the Empire of Art values art and other fields of activity equally. Because the Empire of Art looks after the Boarding House we call Earth, and its happiness—which comes from forests, rocks, wells, rivers, and human wonderment. The Empire's reproduction was very solid the day Jagger reported that the UN were going to allocate 200 billion dollars per year, gathered from developed countries, as much as they could afford.

—I smell, said Paul McCartney, our smell this day: it is the smell of a warm, small eaglet. Our Empire's rank is very positive.

—After Peter Henke's health improvement, said Mick Jagger, I smell the fragrance of a rose, which has been amplified by the sort of amplifiers I use at gigs in the world's biggest stadiums.

—Okay, said Annette. You are invited to a ball, and you can try some Lithuanian pizza. Lithuanians are not some sort of wops, although Mussolini, he was tough.

McCartney was just a Colonel in love, which Annette knew, particularly when she felt the heat of an amorous gaze from that General of courtly love, Mick Jagger.

Meanwhile Sean was getting upset, starting to believe that Annette will never show him any attention. Who was he, after all? A *kiokushinkai* black belt owner? He didn't lay claim to his father's achievements.

He had enough sense to realise that in competitions for love, youth was not necessarily a trump card. A worthy rival could be three times older than him.

Paul McCartney had been thinking all day about an anonymous letter brought by a Yellow Brigade patrolman. There it was written that Sean Lennon was in love with Annette and was seeking her hand. But that was not all that was written in the letter. Worst of all, it said that on Wednesday when Paul was in England, his place in Annette's ward was taken by Mick Jagger. The anonymous letter added that Jagger had not been wasting his time idly.

Item: happiness.

I'm happiest, says Annette, when on a hot day I dive in the water and feel the cold water on my spine and my necks, and when I drink juice with ice on a hot day, and I get comfortable in an automobile that has an air conditioner.

Memory.

Mick's biggest misfortune during the emigration project was a stretched ligament. Going across the street Mick stretched a ligament in his right foot. A Caritas nun bound his foot, but his foot hurt every time he moved it, and Mick became irritable and started snapping at Charlie's every word. This injury made him realise the value of studying karate, with its emphasis on the supremacy of will. For a whole month he did not do any fencing at the English Club. Prince Charles and David Bowie missed him and made phone calls inquiring after him.

Item: love.

One time McCartney was so crazy with love that he climbed up into the tower of a castle—much visited by tourists and wrote: Annette + Mick = ?

A big pain was gnawing at McCartney. Annette was one of the biggest loves of his life. However, as people mostly look forward, not backward, it seemed to him that he had never been so deeply in love. But the anonymous letter mentioned two rivals: Sean and Mick.

Paul knew, that as part of a team with John Lennon he had been more creative. But as if Annette, a woman, would be concerned about that? He scratches his head, wondering how he will bear the envy and how he will protect this precious jewel—Annette. In the category "Love, Friendship, Sympathy", Annette was at the top, in his life. He did not have the combative traits that were evident in John and Mick.

The anonymous letter had stabbed Paul's gentle heart and it was bleeding profusely.

The hippy slogan of 'love, freedom and peace', his generation's foundation, trembled from envy, which is typical of every sensitive person.

In theory, Annette should even be able work as a prostitute, but still have someone special, or even a few special people, whom she held in higher esteem than all the others. A prostitute can be loved, and she can be in love. Paul understood that well, but his heart was troubled by feelings of proprietorship. And now the confrontation with Jagger. The latter had slithered in like the serpent in the Garden of Eden.

—What are you doing here with that weakling? Jagger asked Annette.

—Do you play bass guitar? Paul asked. Like you did with Brian Jones.

—Oh yeah, and what did you do with Lennon? Mick raged.

—*Yesterday* and *Hey Jude,* pronounced Paul, pensively.

—*I can't get no Satisfaction*, pronounced Jagger, pensively.

—*Girl, girl,* Paul said, and began to caress the Siamese twin's feet.

—*Lady Jane,* Lady Annette, said Jagger.

—In the end, why argue? said Annette. Just try out your strength like gentlemen, with swords.

—Your voice is a gift of nature, not of the mind, said Mick.

—Oh big deal, your stretched vowels, said Paul. Very well then, let's fight

—Sean, bring the rapiers. We are duelling, said Jagger.

In the television and recreation room, space was made by pushing the tables to the edges, and the spectators and fans sat on them. Zurab Mšvidobadze himself turned up, carrying a first aid kit.

A lunge forward—a jab. Jagger deflects. A lunge forward—a jab. McCartney deflects.

Someone turned on the TV. It was showing a program about the problem of providing clean water to people, which is going to be a big problem in this, the third millennium. Meanwhile, in the middle of the floor there was a duel going on between two rockers, whose creations will probably be popular throughout the third millennium.

The left-handed McCartney used his advantage and pressed Jagger. Suddenly with a leap to the side and a descending blow, Jagger knocked Paul's rapier out his hand, performing what judoists call an 'accost', sticking his weapon against the prostrate McCartney's throat.

—She is mine, said Jagger.

—No, she is mine, said McCartney.

—OK, I'll compromise, said Jagger. She is ours.

—Ok, she is ours, said McCartney. He wanted to live.

***

(Written by Jurga Ivanauskaitė)

The hard-working McCartney was exercising the solfeggio that morning; he wrote two songs and spent one hour choosing a wedding suit.

That lion of high society, Mick Jagger, almost wore out his nose trying to choose perfume for the bride. He wanted Annette to smell nice, the way he liked her to smell.

Charlie Watts said that to him this scene had the odour of Arabian trotters' manure, i.e. fascinating.

And here we are at the steps of Munich cathedral.

A group photo is being made. The German Pope has given special dispensation for Annette to marry Paul McCartney and Mick Jagger: one bridegroom for each of her heads.

Instead of Mendelssohn's Bridal March, the music played was a couple of the best Beatle numbers and a couple of the best Rolling Stones numbers.

There were more than a few Lithuanians at the wedding.

Suddenly Ivan Ivanovich Ivanov burst in past the people and the Yellow Guard.

—Blast your eyes! some Lithuanians cursed him.

The young ones jumped on him. A large Finnish knife was jabbed into his left eye.

***

(Written by Jurga Ivanauskaitė)

Gallows, campfire, Keith Richards and a Russian-speaking Grim Reaper telling the story.

The girl, who had gone out into the world looking for horror, was full of awe.

—Let me finish the story, may I? she asked.

—Why not? said Keith. You continue.

—I'll end the story, because I would like to go home to Mother. I'm horrified! But I'm happy! I got a real fright! I got to experience real fear!

They all started dancing around the campfire. Even Ivan Ivanovich Ivanov, with the Finnish hunting knife still embedded in his left eye socket.

***

—Well, how was it?— he asked the girl. —Was it horrible?

—Not so horrible as would leave you gasping, but quite OK.— she replied.

Maybe that's what you say too?

***

99